I0639571

Frey Lope Felix de Vega Caprio, F. W. Cosens

Castelvines y Monteses.

Tragi-comedia

Frey Lope Felix de Vega Caprio, F. W. Cosens

Castelvines y Monteses.
Tragi-comedia

ISBN/EAN: 9783744786973

Printed in Europe, USA, Canada, Australia, Japan

Cover: Foto ©Andreas Hilbeck / pixelio.de

More available books at **www.hansebooks.com**

CASTELVINES Y MONTESES.

TRAGI-COMEDIA.

BY FREY LOPE FELIX DE VEGA CARPIO.

TRANSLATED BY F. W. COSENS.

LONDON:

PRINTED AT THE CHISWICK PRESS.

FOR PRIVATE DISTRIBUTION.

1869.

INTRODUCTION.

M R. J. O. Halliwell kindly lent to me some time since a copy of " Romeo and Juliet, a Comedy written by that celebrated Dramatic Poet, Lopez de Vega, contemporary with Shakespeare, and built upon the same story on which that greatest Dramatic Poet of the ENGLISH Nation has founded his well known Tragedy : London, printed for William Griffin, at Garrick's Head in Catherine Street, Strand; 1770" [Price 1s.]. 8vo. pp. 30.

Knowing something of Lope de Vega's " Castelvines y Monteses," I was interested to learn how the anonymous translator had treated his original ; upon referring to the text I found that, in addition to the alteration of the name of the play, the dramatis personæ had all been rechristened, so that Castelvines were printed Capulets, and Monteses, Montagues, the Roselo Montes of Lope de Vega, Romeo Capulet, and Julia Castelvin Juliet Montague; further examination resulted in the discovery that the translator, " To render his work more familiar to the English reader, has printed it under the title of the English Play, from which it scarcely differs in anything except the catastrophe and some scenes that have no manner of connection with the main subject ; these scenes indeed occur frequently, and for that reason the editor has not translated the Spanish comedy from beginning to end, but contented himself with giving a general plan of Lopez de Vega's piece and a translation of such scenes only as answer to others in Shakespeare's tragedy."

Here follows a specimen of the " general plan " :—

" These two old gentlemen, the heads of the Capulet faction, come forward and declare they should both be charmed to see their children smitten with each other, because they propose to make a match between them. Things don't succeed quite to their mind ; Octavio falls in love with Juliet, but Juliet does not like Octavio, and contents herself with returning him a polite answer."

Lope's poetry is thus treated :—

JULIET.

" Did you remark that young gentleman who talked to me ? What a charming youth, my dear Celia, and how happy must the woman be who attaches him to her ? "

Such appearing to me eminently unsatisfactory,

and a very traitorous rendering of the original, I have attempted a more faithful translation of the complete play.

To those interested in Shakespeariana it may be of value to note how two great contemporary dramatists treated the same story for the stage.

It is to be regretted that the work has not been undertaken by other than an amateur hand, being worthy a better fate, but unfortunately the fact remains that it could never prove commercially profitable to a competent translator or publisher.

I have chosen the best available text, that of Don Juan Eugenio Hartzenbusch, a most carefully collated edition, and published by Rivadeneyra in his Biblioteca de Autores Españoles, Madrid, 1860.

F. W. C.

Thornton Road,
   Clapham Park,
    March, 1869.

ERRATA.

At foot of page 29, *for* " here the MS. is illegible," *read* " some lines are wanting."

At page 33, line 13, *for* " now" *read* " not."

CHARACTERS REPRESENTED.

ROSELO.	RUTILIO.
OTAVIO.	BELARDO
ANSELMO.	LORETO.
ANTONIO.	*A Captain.*
TEOBALDO.	*Gentlemen.*
ARNALDO.	*Soldiers.*
COUNT PARIS.	*Musicians.*
LORD OF VERONA.	*Servants.*
MARIN.	*People.*
CELIO.	JULIA.
FABIO.	DOROTEA.
FESENIO.	SILVIA.
LIDIO.	CELIA.
LUCIO	TAMAR.
FERNANDO.	*Ladies.*

The Scene is in Verona, Ferrara, and in other parts.

CASTELVINES Y MONTESES.

ACT I.

SCENE I.—*Street in Verona.*

ANSELMO, ROSELO, *and* MARIN.

Anselmo.

HE house is all ablaze,
 The noise of revel fast and furious.
  Roselo. Some son or daughter weds, may-
   hap.
  Anselmo. No doubt a wedding or be-
   trothal feast.
 Roselo. Marin, go, enter thou, and see thy looks
Be guarded, and thy tongue discreet.
 Marin. And for my pains to clear the scraps
From off the dirty platters they have left,
Shall I go venture 'mid our deadliest foes,
That I may tattle of the sight?
 Roselo. Who, thinkest thou, will ever care
To note thy entrance or thy exit there?

B

Marin. Dark deeds have ever witnesses at hand.
This hated house of Castelvin—
　Roselo. Thy chicken's heart doth fail thee, then, Marin.
　Marin. Bah! would that all Castelvin's brood were here,
And each with temper'd blade unsheathed!
I, with my cloak and rapier keen,
Would single-handed show
What deeds mine own good arm
Could compass at a stretch.
But to be trapp'd behind the closed doors
Seems but at best a currish misadventure.
　Anselmo. If, then, thy fancy leads thee on
To look upon this wedding rout,
And join Castelvin and his merry guests,
Go, don thy mask, and enter boldly in,
As one who claims Castelvin blood or kin.
　Roselo. Some risk of question—
　Anselmo. Nay, nay! who'll seek to question thee,
Or care to know thy business there.
　Roselo. Come, then, Anselmo! let us in.
I'd look upon these merry maids.
　Anselmo. And find a paradise of fair women,
Where danger lurks for heart and life
I' the liquid motion of a lady's eye.
Thy father leader of the Montes is,
And will not brook within his walls
The name Castelvin or his kin,
Or he doth rage as one with crazéd tongue.
Antonio, in whose house this revel rings,
Is, as thou know'st, chief of Castelvin's band,
And a deep hater of the house of Montes.
　Roselo. And yet is heaven passing just, to give

To Montes men the valour, while
Castelvin's women are so fair, you'd say
The die which seraphims did stamp
Had moulded each ;—
These feuds, methinks, should end by wedding torch.
Then would Italia envious be
Of brave Verona's chivalry.

   Marin. I, not only as Verona's son, but man,
Am troubled, bored, and plagued to see
The ills this cankered hatred breeds ;
The very dogs do snarl and bite,
As, wandering up and down your streets,
They by Castelvin's or Monteses' men are held.
Each varlet struts with muzzled hound in leash,—
Free, and their teeth were swords,
What work they'd give the Alguazils !
Your cats with discords music hail,
Companions of the Montes' or Castelvins' kin ;
Scratching in kitchens low, on house-flats high,
They spit and claw as they were flesh and blood.
Then come the cocks, who stately strut and crow
In rival bands, and ever live at war ;
For let a cock of Montes' brood but crow,
Thirty Castelvines rush to dizzy heights,
And crack their throats in chorus.

   Roselo. Thy tongue, Marin, scarce matches with thy wit ;
And yet some wisdom holds thy nimble tongue.

   Marin. Thy word and deed a match unseemly and
       unwise;
Thou seek'st to enter yonder palace gate: you know
There every man's thy sworn and deadly foe ;
And will revenge upon our luckless heads

The ills they've ever known or thought.
Should my advice deter from such mad freak,
I'd say my words held wit and wisdom too.

    Roselo. Thanks, good Marin, but I must even have
Mine own free fancy unmolested go,
Despising that which men call easy gain,
I'd climb a much more cragged path.
Anselmo, if thou think'st my fancy crazed,
Bear with me in my folly.
Annul for once thy humour sage,
And help me in my mad one.
I know thou think'st this freak most rash,
And one which courts both bloodshed and dismay;
But come, let's don our masks and cloaks,
And enter where the shadows thickest fall,
That so, unheeded, we may feast our eyes,
And note the blithsome dancers in disguise.

    Anselmo. Our masks and dresses will good passports be.
Come, then; I see the storied beauty of the dames
Hath fired thy quick-pulsed blood.

    Roselo. Seeing not, I fain would see,
So senseless folly thrusts on me.

    Anselmo. I believe this folly fits thy fancy well.

    Marin. Now I do wager ye will both return
With discontent upon your faces writ.

    Roselo. Wishes are whetted by the dangers hid;
I long for pleasures prudence doth forbid.

SCENE II.—*Garden of the house of* ANTONIO.

ANTONIO, TEOBALDO, JULIA, DOROTEA, CELIA, OTAVIO,

Cavaliers, Ladies, and Musicians.

Antonio. The heat within oppresses much ;
Here 'twere better that we rest.

Otavio to Julia. I, sweet cousin, find oppression here
As great as that within.

Julia. Wanting a pert lover, thou, good coz,
Would'st favour me.

Otavio. More need have I of favours, coz.

Julia. Of all these gay and joyous maids,
Hath none a smile or dance for thee, Otavio ?

Otavio. I seek them not.

Julia. Why leave their smiles unsought, good coz ?

Otavio. I have no wish to seek, for where I seek,
My seeking is but hopeless search.

Teobaldo. Come, come, Antonio, let us rest awhile.

Antonio. Where stay our children ?

Teobaldo. Ah me ! 'twould be a happy day for us,
That sees fair Julia wed Otavio.

Antonio. They're cousins, true ; but if concerted well
'Twould be most easy.

Enter CELIO *and* FABIO, *two maskers.*

Celio. Have we the licence here to dance ?

Antonio. Why not, if you so wish it, sir ?

Fabio. What measure will you please to dance ?

Celio. But one, a measure in a certain lady's sight,
A single glance, a flash from whose soft eyes,
Would echo in my heart, and seek at once
Fruition on her rosy lip.

Enter ROSELO, ANSELMO, *and* MARIN, *masked.*

Anselmo. Here do the maskers seek the air,
And ever here.

Marin. Yes, ever here is language of the dance.

Roselo. Hush, fellow, moderate thy voice !

Anselmo. Already have they danced some rounds,
And now for converse calm seek the cool air.

Roselo. Oh, wondrous beauty ! in deed and truth
Thou a Castelvine's heavenly seraph art ;
And I since birth have ever schooled been
To hate and curse thee.

Anselmo. Now which of beauty beareth off the palm ?

Roselo. She in whose ear yon fellow whispers,
And by her side as 'twere enchanted stands.

Anselmo. Speak, man : enchain her ear thyself.

Roselo. How ugly has Otavio grown !

Anselmo. Roselo, see, thou hast removed thy mask.

Roselo. I heed it not, nor care who sees my face.

Anselmo. Replace it, man, at once, or we—

Roselo. 'Tis most treacherous thus to steal
Within this good man's house, and masked ;
I 'll face them boldly, as I am.

Anselmo. Come hence; e'en now thou courtest observation.

Roselo. I am, and ever have been from my birth
A careless, wild, and silly fool, a stupid clod of earth.

Anselmo. What misadventures may your folly breed!
Antonio aside to Teobaldo. What! Bearded thus within
  the sacred walls of home?
Roselo Montes in my house!
 Teobaldo. Hush, listen!
 Antonio. To what? to whom? I—
 Teobaldo. To one now cooler than thyself.
This youth a noble nature doth unfold,
Though but of thoughtless age he is;
He knows no venom of that cursed hate
So madly cherish'd by our rival kin,
And seeing that we joyous revels hold,
He boldly comes to share them.
 Antonio. Some false intent he hath.
If he be arm'd, methinks he aims at treachery.
 Teobaldo. Thy reason prompted not those words.
He comes in boyish confidence and truth,
And as for swords, our kinsmen here
Do fill the garden now on every side.
 Antonio. Base outrage on our name and blood!
 Teobaldo. Antonio, as an honour treat it.
 Antonio. I judge not thus this most unseemly deed;
He dies a traitor's death.
 Teobaldo. Then will I not aid thee
In such a coward deed; he comes
As gallant goshawk to the quarry flies,
To see what pretty flutterers, taking wing,
Do sigh and wish for mates.
Keep thine own counsel, and no tumult raise;
Nor fire the heated blood of kinsfolk here.
 Antonio. My blood is hot, and yet
Some prudence doth thy counsel entertain.

Teobaldo. Give my grey hairs full credit, then ;
And if thy daughter be in presence here,
Is not also mine ?

   Antonio. For all sakes, then, I will be calm.

   Teobaldo. I do but counsel as cool prudence guides.

   Anselmo. What moves you thus—why gaze with such
      intent ?

   Roselo. Methinks dark death doth yonder point.

   Anselmo. But gazing thus
With tender look and contemplation keen
Doth give occasion to Castelvin's kin
To draw their swords upon us.

   Roselo. Their swords, their looks, or hate
To me are naught.   O Love! sweet Love!

   Anselmo. Love ? they'll call thy rashness
By another name.

   Roselo. Stand thee aside, Anselmo ; let me gaze
On that pure heavenly maid 'till eyesight fails ;
Then let all evils hap that may
Such as this hated house doth crave,
And if it is that life itself be forfeit
For such a glorious heaven as this, Anselmo,
Who cares to breathe the air of this dull earth ?
I'd welcome death a thousand times ;
For if these Castelvines' daughters slay
Like basilisk with fatal blighting gaze,
Who would not joy to look and end his days ?

   Anselmo. I marvel not to find thy fancy touch'd,
Such beauty lacks but halo of the saint,
So softly doth it steal upon the sight.

   Roselo. Is she not lovely ?

   Dorotea to Julia. What a handsome youth is that ? look ;
Mark you his presence, Julia ?

Roselo. When fear should fast my tongue in silence bind
Then is my love all kindled and ablaze.
Anselmo, speaking for myself.
How dare I whisper sweet discourse in ear
Of one who hates all Montes and their kin ?

Anselmo. Wise words, Roselo : and may thou
Think ever thus !

Julia. If ever Love in masquerade should come
And so disguise himself and yet peep forth,
Methinks 'twould be with such a form and face
As that of yonder gentle youth, all grace.
Ah me ! methinks 'tis Love himself,
Who, craving thus a silly maiden's heart to wound,
Seeks in such guise to slay.

Roselo. Great Heaven, why a Montes I ?
Why not Castelvin born as yon sweet maid ?
For such a birthright would I barter heaven's joy,
And name, and kin. Ah, Cupid, ruthless boy !

Julia. Amid the flowers of this fertile earth
Methinks the welcome showers of spring have wept
This bright Narcissus into life.

Roselo. If this indeed be Paradise, who cares
For hostile houses' hatred or revenge ?
Mayhap 'tis Hades, and 'tween love and hate
Yon seraph shape angelic holds her state.
Fool, dullard that I am ! so rash, so weak ;
And yet I'd even venture more, and speak.

Julia. Oh, that he would but deign a whisper'd word,
I'd be so gentle, staid, and courteous ; seek
To please him so. Back, hot blush, from cheek !

Dorotea. In conversation now doth Julia hold Otavio
While yonder mask approaches.

C

Roselo. 'Tis love that blinds me, bids me hope and fear ;
And yet 'tis love that makes me bold while here.

Julia. Ah, fond youth, were I that happy maid
Whose only life and hope might be
To bask in sunshine from those tender eyes !

Dorotea. He comes ; and, I am sure, intends
To seat himself beside me, yet I fear.

Julia. I would he cared to rest beside me here.

ROSELO *sits on one side of* JULIA, OTAVIO *on the other,*
ANSELMO *sits by* DOROTEA *on another bench.*

Otavio to Julia. It must have been most fit to love,
That I should know what joy it is to love,
And so a rival moth-like braves the flame ;
But all his tender looks are vain, she's mine.
The garden may be trimm'd and fresh,
But not for him this flower ; he seeks but shall not find,
While I must be alert, though Cupid may be blind.

Roselo to Julia. Lady, it seems great boldness of my part
To seat me here beside Verona's Queen—
Yet may you well forgive the deed,
For all the fascinating fault's thine own.
So, sweetest lady, blame me not, I pray,
But rather that rare beauty which enchants
And bids me thus be venturesome and rude ;
For the bright pure light which laughs
Within those heavenly eyes and curls around thy lip
Hath lured me, like the moth, to flaming fire.
Enchanted thus I die, fluttering i' th' flame ;
Yet am I bold like Phaethon, daring suns
Which lighten on to drifting death.
Sweet lady, daring thus I'd die,

Rather than live unloved by thee ;
For if thine eyes dare deign to slay,
I'll e'en gladly brave cold death to-day ;
But first, oh, let me tell how much I love,
In that I feel, alas ! I can but mortal be,
And ere I die would whisper 'tis for thee.

   Julia aside. What tender words this masker speaks.
   To Otavio. I fear thy reasons are all feign'd.
   Otavio. Who speaks of reason ? mine
Was long since hushed to sleep by love.

   Roselo. As a masker and a guest I'm here,
Otavio, and if too bold to take this seat,
The heat within doth drive me hence,
If thou carest here to sit, I'll rise.

   Otavio. As it may please you, sir.
   Julia. Sit one on each hand, as now ;
And if it be the heat ye fear, why then,
As thou, Otavio, this side chills,
So can I coldly chill again, until
Our masking friend be ice.

   Otavio. Cousin, what unseemly words are these !
   Julia. Be kind and gentle to a stranger, coz ;
To thee, such matters matter not, I know.

   Otavio. Thus ever wilt thou cross my love ;
Aside. {I dare not lose my treasure, or
      {I would some words provoke ;
I'd have thee speak as Lady Julia should.

   Roselo. An the fault be mine, sweet Lady, I
Will hence at once.

   Julia. And, prithee, whither ?
   Roselo. Within to join the dance.
   Julia. Here, then, the pastime's poor ?

Roselo. Nay, lady, 'tis heaven by thy side ;
But if I be uncourteous—

Julia. No discourtesy can rest with one
Who pleading finds such gentle words as thine.
(*Aside to Roselo.*) He on my right I hope grows weary,
And mayhap will leave us.
(*To Otavio.*) Sit closer to my side.

Otavio. Ever when I nearer come—why then
Thou turn'st thy face away again.

Julia. You soon turn choleric, uncourteous coz,
But I would speak in serious mood.

Otavio. Ah, then indeed I am repaid,
The anger which I felt is gone, sweet maid.

JULIA *gives her hand to* ROSELO, *but turns her face to*
OTAVIO—ROSELO *understanding that her conversation
is addressed to him.*

Roselo. Oh! sweet, soft hand, to clasp so close in mine.

Julia. I hope to please thee, gentle coz,
And yet I fear my boldness doth do more
Than much outstep all maiden modesty.
I can show thee no greater favour than
To say thou hast my most enduring love.

Roselo. He who is primed to drink a toast
To Love, needs little invitation to the deed.

Julia. He who doth turn a shoulder to the foe
Surrenders at discretion.

Otavio. Yet when thou turned'st from me
And left mine enemy to gaze upon thy face,
Think'st thou 'twas strange to doubt ?

Julia. And so I show my hate and doubt,
By leaving all for thee.

Otavio. Sweet lady Julia, now no longer
I complain nor doubt.

Roselo. Dare I give credence to mine ear
That these sweet words are all for me?

Julia. Lack I not some courtesy, good coz?
And yet I see no help for't.

Otavio. Nay, Julia, thou wouldst never err
Though placed by Love in greatest strait.

Julia. And thanks you owe so much to me,
And yet thou think'st so little due to be.

Otavio. Julia, would'st thou drive me mad?

Roselo. She favours me beyond compare.

Julia. Did opportunity permit, you'd see
How bold and saucy I would be.

Otavio. Good Fortune smiles upon my hopes.

Roselo. Her words fall on my ravished ear
As murmuring waters flowing near.

Otavio. Thus joy doth follow small mishap.

Roselo. She speaks to me alone while yonder fool
Doth think each whispered word 's for him.

Julia. Oh, never in these sweet sunny hours of life
Knew I so much to charm me.

Otavio. Sweet love consumes me
With his thousand fires.

Roselo. Each honied word her lip distils
Creeps in mine ear as most melodious music thrills.

Julia. Think ye not, sirs, such free and open speech
Doth savour of some licence.

Otavio. Love like ours, sweet coz, doth know
Full liberty of word and thought.

Roselo. Deem me not rashly bold nor rude ;
But as I saw and madly loved, so thou
Dost heal the wound with charmèd words.

Julia. To see thee was to love. I blush,
For art thou not so handsome, bold,
So young and gallant too ?

Otavio. Having thy love, I breathe, sweet coz,
The air with angels.

Julia. I'll say thou art a mirror, where
Though I am far distant from the sun,
His glorious rays shall fall on thee,
And by reflexion glance on me ;
And so thy light and heat remain as part of mine.

Roselo. The sun's great brightness burns apace
Because I feel him at the full ;
And yet undazzled still I see my sun of love,
No shadows now I fear from clouds above.

Julia. A question, who doth love me best ?

Otavio. I !

Roselo. I !

Julia. Whose then am I ?

Otavio. Mine !

Roselo. Mine !

Julia. Wilt thou be mine only ?

Otavio. Yes !

Roselo. Yes !

Julia. And wilt ne'er forswear me ?

Otavio. No !

Roselo. No !

Julia. Carest thou to see me oft ?

Otavio. When can I see thee ?

Roselo. When can I see thee ?

Julia. Later, then 'tis better.

Otavio. Better!

Roselo. Better!

Julia. Say then who shall guide thee?

Otavio. Love!

Roselo. Love!

Julia. Wilt come alone?

Otavio. I will!

Roselo. I will!

Julia. Shall I wait for thee?

Otavio. Wait!

Roselo. Wait!

Julia. May I come assured?

Otavio. Assured!

Roselo. Assured!

Julia. Where?

Otavio. The orchard!

Roselo. The orchard!

Julia. Be silent, Love.

Otavio. As death.

Roselo. As death.

Otavio. Methought that echo, with her twice-told voice,
Did whisper'd answer give to every utter'd word.

Julia. 'Twas naught but roaming fancy's flight
Or zephyrs whispering to the starry night.

Roselo to Julia. Not one single word mista'en.

Otavio. Thy rashness, sweet, aggrieves me not,
Thy misgivings cause me no surprise ;
Echo I'd have repeat the voice I love,
Ever in whispers to the crowd unheard.

Julia. If the whispers be not thine,
Whose then their echo? The words

Thou heard'st perchance were mine.

Otavio. Sweet Julia, I'd have our lives to be
Naught but the echo of thy love for me.

Antonio. Time draws on apace,
Already it is growing late.

Julia, aside, (*giving a ring to Roselo*). Keep this.

Otavio. Keep this! keep what?

Roselo (*aside to Julia*). Oh, this indeed is bliss,
What do I not owe thee, sweetest maid?

Julia to Otavio. How dull thou art!
Dost comprehend me yet, or only part?

Otavio. Nay, how should I?

Julia. Didst thou not note that thus
I placed my hand upon my heart
In token that I gave it free to thee,
And so I said, in truth, keep this.

Otavio. So will I, my soul's idol, and for ever
Guard thy precious gift of love.

Roselo (*aside*). Is she not angelic as discreet?
Amazed I listen to her words so sweet;
She bids me this dear ring to guard,
And so her heart surrenders all to me.
Otavio thinks 'tis his. Oh Love! blind boy,
Her beauty and her wit enslave. Oh joy!

Antonio to Teobaldo. Thy words indeed were wise
And most discreetly turn'd.

Teobaldo. I did but counsel apt discretion now.
Come, it grows late apace, we'll in;
Already dance and revel cease.

Antonio. Torches, ho! torches, here.

Teobaldo. Farewell, and heaven guard and keep thee;
To-morrow we will speak of this again.

Dorotea. Good night, my sweet and loving coz.

  Julia. Heaven have you in safe keeping, coz,
And so farewell.

Exeunt. JULIA *and* CELIA *remain ; as* ROSELO *passes
          out he exchanges glances with* JULIA.

  Julia. Stay, Celia, stay, I'd speak with thee anon—
  Celia. And I, my lady, too, have much to say.
  Julia. Did'st ever see such loving eyes ?
Did'st note the one that spake ? ah me !
His words indeed were sweet !
    Celia. And does my lady Julia know his name ?
    Julia. No, but I'd tell him 'mid a thousand men,
Those loving eyes did so enslave mine own.
I fear I play'd the wooer,
So bold and blushless, so unmaidenly was I.
But I have heard it said that men
Have eyes for holidays as well as coats ;
And, slipping on such saints day garb—
Until the haughty maid droops eyelid down—
    Celia. And then—
    Julia. This youth he hath so charm'd my heart,
Already it grows sad and restless when apart.
    Celia. A rare cast, madcap, hast thou made !
But court not the witching that thy fancy coins
This gentle youth doth charm the men,
And in Verona he is ever known to be
The soul of honour and of manly truth.   Ah me !
And all the women love him too.
So take good heed, sweet lady mine,
Lest that thou love thine own perdition ;
For this Roselo is Arnaldo's son,

Lord of the house Montesi.

Julia. Oh, Celia! say not so ; oh, grief! oh, tears!
Oh, misery and woe!

Celia. Dear lady, moderate thy grief, I pray,
'Twere better to advise thee, knowing all,
That thou may'st guard in time, thy madness see
While yet the power to guard remains to thee.

Julia. How can I guard, for in most wanton haste,
I gave mine hand, and he did take it?
How dared a Montes step within
The home and house of Castelvin?

Celia. I heard them whisper, now without,
God grant they kill him not, rash youth,
As forth he sallies through our portals to the street.

Julia. Hush! hush! methinks I hear—
But no! Great God, protect him!
I'll mount the stair, and from the window look
He—he—no!
'Tis nothing! is my brain all fire?—
Ah, there he goes, alone and safe!

Celia. Two others follow, and the one I see is Teobaldo,
And I know
He will protect Roselo Montes well.

Julia. Why came he here—why venture forth?
What madness! and having madly come
Why put aside his mask? that all might see.
Had he not done so, then
My father would have 'scaped offence,
And I,—and I, a hopeless love.

Celia. The greater madness, lady, is
To say thou lovest him.

Julia. I should, I know, respect mine honour much

Before my love ; oh, cruel tyrant ! yet gentle Montes still
For my mischance once seen—Love conquer will.

   Celia. What honour, lady, hast thou chanced ?
For when he sat thou turn'dst aside, and spake
But to Otavio.

   Julia. I but to Otavio spake ; oh, shame !
Oh heaven, rain salt tears ! so Montes is his name.

   Celia. Sweet lady, why so sad ?

   Julia. Sad, more than sad ; oh shame !
For while I lip converse held,
And on Otavio smiled, how dare I tell,
My words were all Roselo's, and oh ! he knew it well.

   Celia. The freedom of the revel doth allow
Such speech, and yet no honour be in question.

   Julia. I gave, oh shame ! I gave a ring.

   Celia. E'en that the freedom of the dance permits.

   Julia. Worse, I did concert to meet this youth
To-morrow night, beneath the shadow of the trees
Which in the orchard grow.

   Celia. Stay thou within, and meet him not.

   Julia. Oh! I cannot, Celia, for I love him so.

   Celia. Forget him, lady, for thy father would
Wed thee much rather to a tawny Moor
Than one of Montes' kin.

   Julia. Had I but known him Montes, how discreet
I would have been ; so wrong, so bold,
Unmaidenly ; and yet if he should come again
His witching voice would vanquish each resolve.
To-morrow, Celia, go thou and seek him early,
And say from me, I have been thoughtless,
Wild, unmaidenly ; and say, and say,
I pray him not to pass this way.

Celia. It shall be done ; and yet, my lady, believe
I feel some pang of heart to see thee grieve,
And find thy maiden fancy touch'd so deep.

Julia. Oh, had'st thou whisper'd wiser
Counsel then.

Celia. His servant always linger'd at my side.

Julia. His servant ?

Celia. Yes, sweet lady, and I swear,
That if the master be so bold, so true
So gallant and so handsome too,
The servant in his place reflects
His master well.

Julia. Much would it please me now to know
Of this same servant that thou namest
If brave Roselo Montes ever loved another.
Seek, good Celia, seek on, till thou find'st,
And tell me truly, for my poor heart's sake.

Celia. Your duty, lady, is but to forget.

Julia. Ah yes, my memory fail'd me for the time !
Tell him how innocent of deceit I was ;
Tell him, oh tell him not to pass this dangerous way :
And yet, I care so much to know
If he doth love another ?   Go, Celia, go.

Celia. This, lady, is but wanting woman's wit.
Let him go love where fancy leads,
He ne'er can wed with thee.

Julia. Woman, how wondrous wearisome thou art,
For ever seeking thus to cross and fret.
What matter is't to thee, if I should care
To know he loved not one but twenty
Of Verona's fairest daughters ?

Celia. To seek to know such secrets is most wrong.

Julia. Again you teaze and vex.

Celia. Come, lady, the hour for bed
The clock hath long since marked.

Julia. I care not yet to rest.

Celia. Shall I Roselo Montes call,
That he may bid thee seek with speed
Those slumbers which thy sleepless eyes so need?

Julia. How sweet to drink his name's sweet syllables.
Place ready for the morrow, Celia, pray,
The dress I yestereven wore,
When I did see my cousin Dorotea.

Celia. Pray heaven, that Roselo Montes be—

Julia. What?

Celia. Thy husband.

Julia. Thou said'st but now that such could never be.

Celia. Love changes never into ever, so
I have heard my grandam say.

Julia. Now thou discoursest sweet and cheering words:
Oh, woman, how discreet!

Celia. I learn this lesson, and do know
No air so fans the ardent lover's flame
As the soft whisper of the loved one's name.

SCENE III.—*Gallery in the house of* ARNALDO ; ARNALDO,
off a journey, and LIDIO.

Arnaldo. Take off my spurs, good Lidio.
- *Lidio.* Good sir, thou seemest out of breath,
Fatigued, and worn.

Arnaldo. The country tires me not so much.
'Tis household cares that to Verona bring me.
But for family and estate,
I fain would pass my life
'Mid country and its solitude !
Here, take my arquebuse.

- *Lidio.* It grieves me that you ever thus do
Come and go alone.

Arnaldo. Look, Lidio, have a care !

Lidio. Is't loaded, then ?

Arnaldo. If that its barrel doth contain
Were housed in heart of Castelvin,
Mine own would know repose enough.
What of my son, Roselo ?

Lidio. Well, very well, heaven be thank'd.

Arnaldo. Does he study ?

Lidio. A little, and he lacks not
Fancies fitted to his age ?

Arnaldo. What ?

Lidio. Fencing, horses, and with tennis ball
And dicing now and then.

Arnaldo. And call you dicing virtuous ?

Lidio. 'Tis thought so in the case of noble blood,

But dice and cards most ugly vices be
Amongst the common herd.

   Arnaldo. By night he sallies forth?

   Lidio. I go to bed so early
That in truth I know not, but
His man Marin and he
Do well agree together.

   Arnaldo. That rogue Marin, I have my fears
He doth not lead him to the church
The preacher's sermons there to hear.
A fort which hath no barbacan
Is easy entrance for a foe.
My son is yet but young ; a boy—
I fear these Castelvines know
That through his eyes I see the light ;
And, choosing the black darkness of the night,
Close mine and his with one sharp stroke ;
For darkness covers treasons with her cloak.

   Lidio. Discharge Marin, the halter
Pulling which they lead him.

   Arnaldo. Think'st thou he'll lack
Another rogue, and one as bad as he ?
For in the case of serving men
I know but one experience.

   Lidio. And that is? . . .

   Arnaldo. The worst who always serves you now ;
And hath he long time served,
Why, then, the master is the man,
And so much more if any secrets known
And locked within his breast there be.

   Lidio. But if the servant be well born, and true
The longer time he serves

The more loyal in his faith he'll grow.

   Arnaldo. Lidio, I fain would make a captive of the boy,
And bind him fast in Cupid's silken chains.
No other prison for such tender years—
Nor one so strong as wedlock's iron bars.
'Tis said that, of its many virtues known,
It giveth brains to thoughtless boys.

   Lidio. With such an arrant knave as this Marin
Still at his side, wedlock will scarce give brains,
And stretching soon may break such silken chains.

   Arnaldo. How, what mean you?

   Lidio. Whatever freedom now he hath
Is but the freedom of untutor'd youth.
But this Marin will lead him
Headlong by the downward path,
E'en after wedded. Where then
His honour, and that of Montes house
Whose unsullied name he bears?
The parents of the lady will dispute,
Some clamorous creditors will their quittance press,
And then the young and trusting wife,
All tears and jealous rage, and pale,
Will fear he loves another;
She lacking, 'mid her jewels rare,
That rarer one named prudence.
He often sups or dines abroad;
And when he's served at home
Is out of humour with the food,
And storms at those who cook'd it.
Then, mayhap, when sunrise tips the hills
He'll seek his couch to rest and sleep,

While she, all bitter tears, doth watch and weep.
And then will bickering be rife, and woe ;
So should he in his anger lay
But finger on his wife, feuds, floutings,
And dishonours dark arise.
Such matrimony is a perjured life,
And man and wife as chainèd galley-slaves
Do go in pairs, and find unhappy graves.

 Arnaldo. Can this Marin such mischief coin ?
 Lidio. Already have I said too much,
And think my counsels sound amiss.
 Arnaldo. Malice is ever found when sought, I know ;
So when some servants nod and shrug,
Speaking soft slanders of their craft,
I then suspect that malice leads,
Or envy cankers in the heart, and breeds.
 Lidio. Such may be known in palaces.
 Arnaldo. Envy a crevice finds in every wall.
 Lidio. So telling all I know and think,
I'm like the judge who rated well and flogg'd
The cheat ; and when the flogging's o'er,
The cheat has stripes and fame to boot,
Some thinking him an injured man.
To thy taste this rogue Marin, this cheat,
May be both good and most discreet.
 Arnaldo. Thy tongue doth wag too fast ;
And I am tired and care not now to answer thee.
 Lidio. Stern truth no answer doth admit,
I confess, yon rogue, I much distrust ;
And I am bound, with loyalty unshaken,
To name the truths I know, however taken.

[Exit ARNALDO.

E

Enter MARIN.

Marin. Hah, worthy Lidio, what's the news abroad ?
Thou household grunter now at home,
What say you to our noble boy ?
What said Arnaldo ; did he not
Question with a thousand words ?

Lidio. A thousand tongues would be too few
For all his words just now : he question'd me
Most closely.

Marin. He spoke of me, how could I doubt it ?

Lidio. Many things he said concerning thee,
My answers were, Take thou no heed ;
With such a master as a tutor, thou
May'st sleep the sleep of trust,
Confiding in such virtue, truth, and wit.
I told him of the counsel that you gave,
And of temptations from his path removed.

Marin. A lucky day it was for me,
When first I press'd thy honest hand,
And in good wine did toast with thee
The fairest damsels of our hearts ;
Whose houses and whose gardens green
We had made our own that day.
And I swear, good Lidio, trusty friend,
That by your caution thou shalt nothing lose.

Lidio. For me enough it is to know
I deal with one of gentle birth,
And one so honest as Marin.

Marin. This very night we'll join a merry crew,
And with guitar and dance will revel at our ease.

Lidio. I'll go see if our old master sleeps,
Meanwhile, get thee in.

Marin. I hold me at your pleasure.

Lidio. From this moment, and for ever,
We are fastest friends.   Farewell.   [*Exit* LIDIO.

Marin. This fellow is the greatest cheat;
An envious, ill conditioned knave;
With dangling rosary and in cassock neat,
He preaches rankest treasons;
But he who cares to live at peace
Within his neighbour's walls,
Must hear and see, but nothing say;
Flatter with lip and eye, be cheery,
And talk, and laugh, and joke;
Small deeds, and use high sounding words.
And though the devil's tongue be long,
He doth not prick it with his tail.
But how to serve, I comprehend; while he
Who deals alone with truth will gain but poverty.

Enter ROSELO *and* ANSELMO.

Roselo. No greater ill could e'er befall a man.

Anselmo. Is such indeed her name
And lineage?

Roselo. Oh! ill assorted beauty, that
Of Antonio Castelvin such seraphim be born.
Oh! fate most cruel and unkind, sad chance,
There's flame-eyed madness in each seraph glance.

Anselmo. Why soughtest thou her house?

Roselo. Marin, Marin.

Marin. Señor, thy father is within.

Roselo. Soon shall he know this maddening love,
Which doth consume my heart.

Marin. Here's crazy nonsense!

Roselo. I feel as if my reason waver'd.

Marin. Know you that the lady is
Of Castelvines' kin?

Roselo. I do, and am undone.

Marin. There is no ill which, taken timely,
But it will yield to cautious cure.

Anselmo. Already are my fears aroused,
Still, if thou wilt but counsel take
All will be well.   Fancy 'twas
The limner's art enslaved thine eye.
Or that in a glass reflected, seen
And, having pass'd along,
Thou findest 'twas a mirror'd dream.

Roselo. I bear her beauty mirror'd in mine eyes,
Her sweet self reflected, and her angel-look
Is ever present to my sight.

Anselmo. To think of loving this Castelvin fair;
'Twould mar thy life; the city too
Aroused would cry out nay.
For, look you, should you pass
By door or window of Castelvin kin
His rapier would be quickly out; the
Very stones would topple on your head.

Roselo. How little dost thou know of love, Anselmo!

Anselmo. What need know more than this,
A bitter quenchless hatred doth divide
Your houses?

Roselo. Yet what befell me, and that beauteous maid ?
Sweet witching words she spake.
　　Anselmo. What ! could'st thou speak
When eyes did only meet ?
　　Roselo. She placed her trembling hand in mine.
　　Anselmo. She might do this, and yet her kin would seek
To kill thee.
　　Roselo. Her rosy fingers placed
This shining ring upon mine hand.
　　Anselmo. Blind eyes in that may even find deceit.
　　Roselo. She bade me in the orchard
Await her coming, and to-night.
　　Anselmo. Then need I say no more
Than this, that orchard green
Will for Roselo Montes be the sward of death.
　　Roselo. Think'st thou so lightly of my love ?
She knew not when she spake
'Twas luring love did beckon.
We saw and loved.
Fear not for me, Anselmo ;
I go well arm'd.   This very night
We meet to hold sweet converse 'neath the trees,
Despite the hatred of our houses.
Hear me, Anselmo ; art thou not my friend ?
And thou, Marin, my servant ?
I yield me to this fond delight,
Madness, delusion, if ye will,
And with me he who loves me well.

＊　　＊　　＊　　＊　　＊　　＊　　＊　　＊　　＊　　＊

(*Here the MS. is illegible for a few lines*).

Anselmo. Although my heart be heavy as a stone,
I'll aid thee, though I face a thousand deaths.

Marin. Am I not most rashly brave? I'll live
And die with thee, my lord, my aid I'll give.

Roselo. Counting such loving help as this,
Mischances may assail ; yet hoping bliss
I count mischances naught,
So little does our prudence weigh
When love the balance trims.
Julia, I swear that thou shalt be mine own,
My truly wedded love, my gentle wife ;
And happy then that day will be
When I may live and die for thee.   [*Exeunt.*

SCENE IV.—*An Orchard.*

Enter OTAVIO, CELIA, *and* JULIA.

Otavio. I understand thee not.

Julia. Nor know I thine intent.

Otavio. Sweet coz, at your command
I'm here.

Julia. Here, how, why?

Otavio. If thou did'st not count upon my coming
Why wand'ring 'neath the stars?

Julia. I came here for no purpose that I know
Save this, to show mine anger if thou cam'st.

Otavio. Thy mem'ry fails, for at the ball,

Thou saidst, we'll meet and here to-night.

Julia. Thou sayest well.   My father rests but ill,
Go thou and lull him to soft sleep ;
And when in slumbers fast he's held,
Come thou and take such poor ungracious love
As I may have for thee ; my father sups above.

Otavio. Wilt thou indeed do this?

Julia. Ne'er hesitate,
I can refuse thee nought.

Otavio. Then will I so contrive, that supper o'er
He shall not ask for thee.

Julia. Here then I wait thy coming, coz.

Otavio. Come dainty sleep, and round him cast
Thy sweet oblivious wings.   [*Exit.*

Julia. Celia.

Celia. Dear lady.

Julia. In so great a strait as this
What can an honest maiden do ?

Celia. While Otavio converse holds within,
Do thou Roselo tell all here,
And truly undeceive him.

Julia. 'Twere deceit so dark to undeceive.
Should I deceive to undeceive ?

Celia. Yes, lady.

Julia. A most cruel sentence this ;
I will to Love appeal.

Celia. How well a woman knows to use
A rival, for the favours she would show
To him she loves the best.   And you well know
Your cousin, now above, doth entertain
Your father at his supper, while you remain

Waiting Roselo Montes here!

Julia. Do I not love, and shall I not deceive?
Otavio should have tied my tongue, nor left
Me here to speak with this Roselo Montes.

Celia. Hush! I hear a footfall near.

Julia. Already had my heart drunk in
The sound.

Celia. He must have mounted by some corded steps.

Julia. How, where could he have fix'd them?
Oh heavens! should he fall!

Celia. I fear me that already he hath fallen.

Julia. If he hath climb'd the wall;
'Tis very high.

Roselo (*without*). Wait thou beneath the wall.

Julia. Oh, had I but my will, brave Montes, now,
No need for envious ladder should there be.

Enter ROSELO *gaily dressed.*

Roselo. Oh, sweetest lady! do mine eyes again
Behold thee? Dear Julia, let me gaze.

Julia. Thou shalt, and with such modesty
As I know well thou hast; 'tis more than mine.
Before thou speak'st thy flatt'ring words,
So apt to cheat a trusting woman's ears,
(For women, if discreet and strong,
Are yet but women after all;
And if they stay to listen, answer will
As women answer, press'd),
I would care first thou heard'st me say
That thou art known to me;
And all my grief is now for what thou art,
And that I fear I am to thee.

But stay! my judgment fails;
For should I curse Monteses' son
I curse Castelvin's daughter too.
When first thou didst entrap my wand'ring eye,
The sight was love,—for doth not all Verona
Full loudly sing Roselo Montes' praise?—
'Twas then I licence gave for words,
'Twas then I own'd myself thy slave;
But, since I know thy name and kin,
My love ebbs back, all chill'd at heart,
Fearing all ills, ay, even dark death's hand.
As gentle blood doth course thy veins,
I dare a favour crave: I do not ask
The ring I gave; I know I sought thy love;
Speak not.
When walking through this street, I pray,
Crouch thee beneath the wall,
So that the shadows hide thee from my sight.
Oh, how I tremble! Farewell, begone,
Leave me. My love it should be hate.
    Roselo. I'll do thy bidding gladly, still
Oh, sweet enemy! sunlight of my soul!
Thou say'st thou hatest, Julia, love;
For me, I cannot hate, I could and will
Return thy ring, rescale these walls;
But not to speak, to say how much I love,
Is more than I dare promise now:
Love without danger loseth strength for strife.
Hear me, sweet Julia! darling! love!
Seeing those dear eyes, hearing that sweet voice,
I loved you, heeding not our kindred's hate,
And when I knew it, then methought

F

'Twere better then to cease to love,
But Love, most fruitful of expedients is,
Holding no ill without its antidote,
Whisper'd, thou canst not cease to love.
In secret if thou wilt ; but love I must,
Oh Julia, mine own sweet Julia !

   Julia. Call me not so oft by name,
I fear my heart will answer, not my tongue.
Thy loving words enchant my soul
And gladden night with sunshine ;
But tell me, since thou will'st to speak,
How found this chance for words ?
Why come, and thus persisting follow me ?

   Roselo. I'd have thee all mine own, sweet star,
In secret, if thou wilt : a close friendship
With a holy friar I have, and he, I know,
Will aid us ; but should his conscience scruples hold,
I'll find some subtle means of cure.

   Julia. My very soul doth tremble at thy words.

   Roselo. What fears my dearest Julia ?

   Julia. More than a thousand ills.

   Roselo. They are but fancied ills ; once wed,
All rivalry would cease, all hatred should be dead.
Love beckons by this safe and secret road
To hold our houses free from hate,
And through our love shall smile everlasting peace.

   Julia. Well did I say thou shouldst not speak ;
But go, lest Otavio come, and find thee here ;
He now in converse doth my father hold.
I know not why I live to love thee so.

   Roselo. Say, sweet one, ere I go, what is thy resolve ?

   Julia. What can I say but this,

That I will go, will meet thee at the church?
And see thou the holy man be there prepared
In wedlock's blessed bonds to bind us;
For since I dared to listen to thy voice,
Like the serpent have I closed mine ears;
So now I close mine eyes as well.
Go, go, I hear approaching footfall!

    Roselo. I go, sweet love, but stay not thou to hold
Much speech, and with Otavio.

    Julia. Look that thou no promise dost forget.

    Roselo. Nay, this I swear, forgetting such.
May heaven desert me at my need.

    Julia. Swear not, for I have read
That ready swearers have
Scant credit with the world or God.

    Roselo. What shall I say, sweet maid?

    Julia. Say that I thy heart's desire am.

    Roselo. They come, sweet girl! Farewell.

    Julia. Carest thou to kiss mine hand?

    Roselo. Yes; but much more, thy lips.

    Julia. Nay, nay! away, my love, begone!

    Marin (without.) Come, master, or I'm off, alone.

                        [*Exit* ROSELO.

ACT II.

SCENE I.—*Exterior of a Church in Verona.*

Enter TEOBALDO *and* FESENIO.

Teobaldo.

AND Dorotea tarries still within?
    Fesenio. She does, and sad at heart enough,
For two Monteses, Donda and Andrea,
Removed her seat aside.
    Teobaldo. Was no Castelvin there?
  Fesenio. One, of all Castelvin's band
The most of settled purpose and command;
Alone he scarce would care to draw,
And more than that, who dares forget
A church's floor is holy ground?
Some small attempt at parley
Did he make, but many Montes, one by one
Came forth, and then most prudent
He gave way.
    Teobaldo. How, gave way?
    Fesenio. In silence, still with sullen scorn.
    Teobaldo. Such silence did the coward prove
Where tarries Dorotea?

Fesenio. Apart ; but she was silent,
And doth desire no fray.

Teobaldo. And so conceded it must ever be,
That all the damsels of Castelvin's kin
Give place to beauteous Montes !

Fesenio. 'Tis hardly wise such bitter sneers
If thou dost hope some steady hand
Shall hold the trembling scales of peace.

Teobaldo (looking in at the door). Seest thou they've cast
      the seats
Upon the ground ?

Fesenio. Carest thou for peace and concord, then
Push not thy revenge so close ;
Dost care that brawls and sword-strife shall
Through all Verona's streets be daily trade ?
For they that brawl shall fell perdition find ;
Wouldst thou breed maddening hate between thy kind ?

Teobaldo. Shall I in silence suffer such a slight ?
Such 'haviour would disgrace a very Goth,
To jostle noble ladies from their seats.

Enter OTAVIO, JULIA, CELIA, *and servants.*

Julia. Thy sister, is she here ?

Otavio. She went abroad some hours since.

Julia. And yet so early !

Otavio. She doubtless thought that thou
Did'st know of this most holy friar's fame,
And so have waited on the sermon more
Early and betimes.

Julia. Hadst thou, good cousin, on last eventide
Declared this to my mother, then I know
We had been long since here,

For she doth love this holy father's counsel.

   Otavio. So many going to and fro, the street
Doth seem alive with moving feet.

      JULIA, OTAVIO, CELIA, *and Servants go in.*

   Teobaldo. Is that my son?
   Fesenio. And the lady I suspect's his cousin.
   Teobaldo. 'Tis somewhat strange!
   Fesenio. Is she not the idol of his heart?
Already they go in.
   Teobaldo. Attend Otavio thou, and say,
I do desire some words with him.
   Fesenio. My Lord, I do thy bidding.   [*Exit.*
   Teobaldo. Disgrace incites, doth urge and tempt,
So much I loathe that hated house.
I did desire a peaceful course,
But then
They had not stung and gall'd me as to-day,
And press'd me hard beyond endurance even,
And yet, thus trusting hasty thought,
Is but
To trim the sail to catch light folly's breath.

      Enter FESENIO *and* OTAVIO *from the church.*

   Otavio. What would my honour'd sire?
   Fesenio. He waits thee here, Señor.
   Otavio. Sir, I stay for thy commands.
   Teobaldo. How, lacking judgment, dost thou move
In matters which affect thy kin;
For daily dangling at thy cousin's heels,
A witless error 'tis to leave to chance

Thy gentle sister, who doth love thee well :
Playing the loutish lover, thou hast miss'd
Both trust and honour in her cause ; ah me !
With Cupid's love-blind eyes, who then can see ?

    Otavio. What great mishap hath cross'd thy will ?

    Teobaldo. Thou 'lt lack no crosses through thy life, my
        boy,
But for thine honour's sake hadst thou been here
By Dorotea's side,
Thou couldst have made some show that Castelvine's blood
Doth flow within thy veins,
And I not be humbled thus to brook an insult from
These proud Monteses.

    Otavio. What insult then hath fallen out to-day ?

    Teobaldo. Had I thy years, my son, thy youth
And strength,
Verona should have seen a quick revenge.
But since my love for thee
Can cure no wound, know this
'Tis Castelvine's honour they offend.

    Otavio. What words are these I hear ?

    Teobaldo. Let not thy hot blood too quickly course,
But listen.

    Otavio. Parley not, for having call'd me coward, fool ;
Say, who is 't thine honour doth offend ?
Speak, speak, I pray !

    Teobaldo. The seats prepared for thy kindred in the church
These craven Montes dared to misplace.

    Otavio. When ? where shall I find the coward crew ?

    Teobaldo. Thou 'lt see them yonder, boy, within.

    Otavio. I will return anon.

    Teobaldo. I did not move thy quick-pulsed blood

That I might play the craven coward here ;
I will go with thee.

    Otavio.   Father, thou shalt not.

    Teobaldo.   I will go in.   *[Exeunt into the church.*

    Fesenio.   That he so madly urge his fiery son
Methinks doth lack a parent's prudence.

Enter ANSELMO *and* ROSELO.

    Roselo.   This way she pass'd, and by her side
Otavio walk'd.

    Anselmo.   So, so, methought it was a summer dream
To be forgotten on the morrow,
For thou in all thy letters nothing wrote
Of Julia Castelvine.

    Roselo.   Who cares to trust on paper thoughts
That burn ; or weary patient friends
With words they would not care to read.

    Fesenio (aside).   And so these are of Montes' house ;
Sad fate should anger bear her bitter fruit !
I will within, and young Otavio seek.

FESENIO *enters the church.*

    Anselmo.   And has Roselo secrets in his love ?

    Roselo.   In good time thou comest to hear my tale ;
'Tis needful I advise you of my love ;
And truly I have much to tell which hath fallen out
Since thou didst journey to Ferrara.

    Anselmo.   All apprehension now I am,
And tremble while I listen.

    Roselo.   That night when thou didst bear
Me company, and I in gladness held
Sweet converse with my love,

Beneath the cedars by the orchard wall
We did agree, upon a certain day
That she, evading all, should come
Alone to church, while I prepared
Should hold Aurelio to our cause,
And that good friar join our hands,
And bless our wedded hopes.
I used such prudence in mine act
As to induce Aurelio to agree ;
Though with strong words he did oppose,
And even begg'd with tears.
Julia with her maid did come
To yonder chapel, with pretence of shrift ;
Aurelio with myself were there ;
And having learn'd our wondrous love,
Did join our hands, and bless us.

   Anselmo. What moonstruck madness hast thou caught ?
   Roselo. Denying us, he saw much chance
Of feeding feuds and nursing noxious hate,
Destruction to Verona's peace.   For had we fled,
Or had I held by force, her name and rights
And mine had been in danger of a thousand ills.
And so we wedded were.

   Anselmo. Better hadst thou said, Roselo,
That death had been thy bride ;
I see no chance of less, when all be known.

   Roselo. With heaven's good help it shall not be.

   Anselmo. 'Tis folly to speak thus, for when
Thou passest down the street by day,
Or seekest thy lady's lattice in the dark,
Or e'en within those holy walls do kneel,
Thou temptest death at every step from Castelvines' steel.

Roselo. Anselmo, here I with due caution move,
And use most sound discretion.

Anselmo. Show me the man who, loving,
Knows or holds discretion worth a thought.

Roselo. I walk but seldom in the street,
And rarely go to mass.

Anselmo. How then see thy wife ?

Roselo. Often and without danger too.

Anselmo. How ?

Roselo. In the soft silence of the dreamy night,
Beneath the orange tree that shades
Her lattice ; and by the cedars dark, I place
A corded ladder strong ; Celia doth wait
While we sweet converse hold.
When day shakes loose her golden locks,
I bid adieu, and by the cords descend,
Where Marin on the watch doth join me ;
And, as the sunlight flashes o'er the hills,
I seek my bed and dream.

Anselmo. In this, then, dost no hazard see ?

Roselo. No, for 'tis done when all Verona sleeps.

Anselmo. Otavio will awake.

Roselo. Otavio loves her, that I know ;
Yet doth her wit delude with outward show.

Anselmo. But how ?

Roselo. Beneath the orchard's walls, from eventide
Till midnight, she speaks and walks with him ;
He then doth bid farewell, and homeward goes
To dream until the morrow sunlight knows.

Anselmo. And this is loving woman's wit !
Hast thou no jealous fear his words
May not be such thy wife should hear ?

Roselo. I often in close ambush lie,
And hear each word.

Anselmo. So thou then art her husband,
And she's thy wife?

Roselo. Those names are ours, and with them
All the joys of wooers' bliss.

Anselmo. I tremble for thy fate.

Roselo. I, love's favourite, tremble not
At aught.

Anselmo. Not even at the bitter hate,
Which doth divide your houses?

Roselo. I nothing fear; for doth not love
And marriage laugh at fear?

Anselmo. I know not now what counsel
Best to give.

Roselo. I'm grateful for thy counsel, but
The deed being done good counsel now
Is but a drop to swell the roaring sea.

Anselmo. What wilt thou do?

Roselo. Patiently I'll wait, Anselmo; for doth not
Patience lift the lowly valleys high,
And tumble lofty mountains down the vale.

Antonio (without). Out, out ye cowards all!
Out, out, Monteses!

Arnaldo (without). Give way, ye knaves, give way!
Death to Castelvines, all!

Roselo. What means this noise within?

Teobaldo (without). Hold not thyself so proudly, or—

Antonio (without). Although thou hast the seats
As high as heaven's vault,
I would, as I do now, seize
And cast them to the lowest hell.

Arnaldo (without). Hold, for thy life!

Antonio (without). Out, out I say, ye coward crew!

Roselo. That voice, it is my father's.

Anselmo. Stand thou here, Roselo.

Roselo. To stand here idly is a coward's choice.

> [*Rushes into the church.*

Anselmo. 'Tis now for life or death.

Enter from the church (with drawn swords) ANTONIO,
    TEOBALDO, OTAVIO, *and* FESENIO ; *who place themselves
    on one side,* ARNALDO, LIDIO, MARIN, *and* ANSELMO *on
    the other ;* ROSELO *in the centre.*

Roselo (apart to ANSELMO*).* Anselmo, go my father
    tell,

And say I hold for Julia's sake alone,

Although my blood denies her kin and house.

Anselmo (apart to ROSELO*).* No need of words, I see

That love doth blind thee.

Roselo. Hold, gentlemen, I pray ; hold

Each hand, I say ; albeit I am a Montes,

And still but young in years,

Yet do I not seek intention'd ill,

And have no care for triumphs

Wrested through revenge.

Touching this hot dispute 'tis well

That reason calmly doth the balance grasp,

And firmly hold thy hands ; meanwhile

Let reason regulate thy words and deeds,

So noble, skill'd and strong for war,

As all Verona knows both Montes and Castelvins are ;

Is then the subject in dispute so grave?

Otavio. Our wounds are those of honour ;
Thy people did offend a daughter of our house.

   Roselo. Tell me, Otavio, how these ills fell out ?

   Otavio (to his followers). They shall die, these proud
      Monteses.

   Roselo. Consider, let us speak apart,
Can justice no amendment make ?

   Otavio. Let all stand back, and thou and I
Will make amends for all this hate.

   Roselo. I have a father here, come let us seek
His counsel, for me, perchance, 'tis love mispent ;
For well I know, I hated am of all
Castelvin's house.

   Otavio. What care we for thy hate, or hope we from thy
      love ?

   Roselo. And yet thou know'st, Otavio, 'tis thy love I
      crave.

   Otavio. Coward !

   Roselo. Otavio, stay ; remember thou that I
Do guard mine honour, as I would
That thou should'st guard thine own ;
Unseemly words—

   Otavio. Was't well that one of Montes' house
Should dare displace the seat
Once set for daughter of Castelvin ?

   Roselo. Sure this may satisfaction seek,
And honour be avenged.

   Arnaldo. 'Twas none that Montes' livery wore.

   Teobaldo. Of what house then were they ?

   Arnaldo. Of Andrea's.

   Roselo. Come, put up your swords
And let us enter now, and I

Will straightway place the seats, from whence
The Montes did remove them.

Otavio. So far the seats, but what
Of words of malice and contemptuous lips?
The sword alone can wipe out stains like these.

Roselo. Such idle words should give no cause
For senseless scuffles in your streets.

Teobaldo. Hast more advice to give?
How his smooth words do chafe and gall.

Roselo. Wed thou Andrea Montes, while I
Will mate with Julia Castelvin.

Otavio. Rather should my life blood flow
And drop by drop creep over these cold stones than I
Would see thee Julia's husband.

Roselo. By such settled purpose every cause
For strife and broil would cease.

Otavio. Villain, defend thyself; provoked
Beyond endurance, I could clutch thy throat
And stab thee, as cowards do defenceless women.

Roselo. Hear all, bear witness of this deed.

Otavio. No need of witness, draw.

Roselo. Gentlemen, ye will all witness hold,
This provocation sought I not;
But that by words of friendship I had hoped
T'avoid this bloody fray.

Otavio. Draw, coward, draw!

Roselo (aside). Oh, Julia mine own love, forgive, forgive.
Out, villain! know, that no coward's arm I own,
One holds me back, who love my soul hath taught,
Otavio, 'tis thou alone this mighty ill hath wrought.

                              [*They fight*, OTAVIO *falls.*

Otavio. I'm hit.

Teobaldo.   Is his wound mortal?

Antonio.   Yes.

Roselo.   Fly, my father, fly.

[*Exeunt* ROSELO, ARNALDO, ANSELMO, LIDIO,
            and MARIN.

Antonio.   Castelvines here!

Teobaldo.   Son—!

Otavio.   Confession!

Antonio.   He murmurs for confession.

Teobaldo.   Oh, misery! oh, woe!

Antonio.   Quick, bear him within the church,
Ere his soul doth wing itself above.

Teobaldo.   And I the cause of all this woe.

[*Exeunt* MONTESES.

TEOBALDO *and the* CASTELVINES *bear the body into the
    church ; the people gradually disperse, murmuring.*

Fesenio.   Teobaldo 'mid this sullen calm hath raised
This sad and senseless storm,
The fatal error then was his.
Let him hope pardon for the wrong, I saw
Roselo did but in due defence of honour draw.

Enter DUKE OF VERONA, *a Captain, soldiers, and people.*

Duke.   Not one in fault shall 'scape alive.

Captain.   Of this event Teobaldo Castelvin alone
Doth bear all blame.

Duke.   And the wounded, count they for much?

Captain.   Many of each rival house.

Duke.   Who slain?

Captain. Otavio, Teobaldo's son.

Duke. Where rests the corse?

Captain. Within the shadow of the sacred cross.
Confess'd, absolved, he meekly died,
His father and his weeping kin beside.

Duke. Who kill'd Otavio?

Captain. Roselo Montes, son
To Arnaldo Montes; all voices say
'Twas Otavio Castelvin provoked the fray
With many bitter words, and so
The deed was one of self-defence, I know.

Duke. Hast thou not some of Montes blood
Flowing in thy veins?

Captain. Of Montes or Castelviñ none,
Nor have I aught of fondness or contempt
For one or other of their houses.

Fesenio. I serve the noble Teobaldo, and I loved
Otavio as a son, for in their house
Since earliest youth I've served;
But in my conscience can I not
Speak of Otavio free from blame;
He did Roselo Montes much provoke,
Who calling all to witness that
He would but guard his threaten'd life,
And strive to keep Verona free from strife.

Captain. Most noble Duke, hast aught
To question more.

Fesenio. Most gracious Duke,
All present should be question'd close.

Duke. Where is Roselo Montes now?

Captain. In yonder tower he refuge finds,
There with his servant, who defends

His master stoutly, hurling stones on those
Who stay below to speak.
  Duke. Roselo Montes, listen !
  Roselo. Who is it calls upon that luckless name ?
  Captain. 'Tis Verona's Duke who speaks to thee.
  Roselo. What would our noble Duke ?
  Duke. Descend in safety ; and my plighted word
Thou hast that none shall let or harm thee.
  Roselo. I yield, confiding in thy princely word.
I dare not strivealone, most noble Duke,
'Gainst all my foes.   I will descend forthwith
And render up my sword to thee ;
Not fairly using which, I would rather die
Of hunger or of fire, than ever yield
To tender mercy of Castelvin's kin.
  Duke. Descend, Roselo Montes, I entreat.
Thou hast my plighted word that none shall dare
To stop or harm thee.
  Roselo. Enough, I come, most noble Duke.
  Marin. Look well you slip not as you go.
  Roselo. Be still :
Marin, I'm guiltless and have naught to fear.
  Marin. Methinks a good wide space the wisest thing
When plaints from notaries to lawyers swing ;
'Tis clanking money or a felon's chain,
The case it may so turn for loss or gain.
Some fellow will most roundly swear
He saw, quite clearly, fifty leagues away ;
Another on his oath declares that night is day ;
Another, that his fancy grows or coins,
All brimming o'er with saids, aforesaids, and the like.
                 [*Exeunt* ROSELO *and* MARIN.

H

Enter JULIA *and* CELIA, *Soldiers and People.*

Julia. Having buried all bright hopes, what care or fear
Of self-respect or honour now.
   Celia. Hush, yonder stands Verona's Duke.
   Julia. What does he here?
Is't to seize Roselo Montes that he comes?
   Captain. Whom have we here?
   Julia. A woman, Julia Castelvin.
   Captain. Thou, then, art daughter to Antonio.
   Julia. One who is daily praying for her death.

Enter ROSELO *and* MARIN, *guarded.*

Roselo. Marin, yonder stands my wife,
The gentle Lady Julia, sweetest life!
   Marin. She'll swear away thy sweetest life.
   Duke. Roselo Montes, didst in hatred slay
Otavio Castelvin?
   Roselo. If he be dead, then did this arm indeed
Without premeditation deal the blow;
Provoked by bitter words I did but draw
My sword in honest self-defence.
   Duke. His gentle cousin in our presence stands,
And one who loved him much.
   Roselo. And I in truth dare ask her, if he fell
In fair and open conflict, ay or no?
   Julia. Most noble Duke, albeit I have lost
A cousin and protector both, a thousand times
I say but yes and yes again, for truth
Doth force these words from out my hapless lips.

Duke. Saw'st thou the fray, fair lady?

Julia. From yonder holy porch, the fray
Was seen of all Verona. This gentleman
Did almost sue for peace;
Otavio, proud and haughty as Castelvin's son
Should ever be, did seek a cause, alas!
For quarrel with this Montes youth—

[*Falls on* CELIA'S *neck.*

Oh, heaven! then my witness is in truth—
I nothing saw through blinding tears.

Duke. What says the damsel
Who with the Lady Julia comes?

Celia. Otavio, sir, since yestermorn did seek
Some cause of quarrel : for, added to his hate,
Some touch of jealousy there dawn'd of late.
Otavio call'd our kinsmen to his side,
Unsheathing then his sword, he raised
The point to this young Montes' heart.
Oh, Duke! oh, lady! I can scarcely speak,
And nothing more I know.

Captain. Those present near the church,
Both friends and foes, do all agree in this.

Julia. No witness then thou hast,
Against Roselo Montes, Duke?

Duke. None. Good captain, what for prudence' sake
Should now mark best our course?

Captain. From out Verona he must banish'd be,
For if he stay a tumult will arise,
And in your streets great danger be
For person and authority.
The Lady Julia is the dead man's kin,
But doth confirm Roselo Montes guiltless

Of this Castelvin's mournful death.
Her servant here affirms the truth of all
The lady hath set forth.

   Duke. Thy counsel doth command our thoughts.

   Captain. Give me thy edict sign'd and seal'd, that I
On pain of death may quell aught leading to a fray.

   Duke. Anon it shall be done.

   Captain. And ere thy will be noised abroad,
Let a strong guard attend, and aid
To give this Montes choice of Rome,
Of Milan, or of Venice as a home.

   Roselo. Most noble Duke, no need of guard,
Mine honour doth command that I obey.

   Duke. With all this tumult now so hot,
'Twere wise to be discreet. Go, Lady Julia,
And we greet you well ; Roselo Montes shall
To our palace hie as honour'd guest.

   Julia. Oh that kind heaven now
Would drag my saddened soul from out
This earthly prison where 'tis chain'd.

   Duke. Unto our palace then, till all
In order of equipment be.

   Roselo. As willing slave, where'er thou wilt.

   Julia. Come, Celia, come, and quickly too,
Lest grief and shame shall hold me in such train,
Where modest maiden dare not safely long remain.

   Celia. Should but these evils end to-day
All may be well. Come, Lady Julia, let's away.

   Roselo. Farewell, sweet Julia, jewel of my soul,
Farewell, sweet sun so bright !

   Julia. Go, or I die, mine eyes' sweet light.   [*Exeunt.*

Enter TEOBALDO *and* DOROTEA.

Teobaldo. Since mine the sin, I can none other blame
For this dark deed of blood.　Oh! misery and shame.

Dorotea. From heaven in my prayers each day
I pray revenge.

Teobaldo, I marvel, weighted with such bitter grief,
I breathe or move; write they of a father, who,
Revengé did higher place than honour true,
Tempting his son to death?　Oh! sad revenge,
Oh! passion, grief, and woe.

Dorotea. All say the blame with rash Otavio lay
In tempting thus to hot contentious fray.
This gentle youth did almost sue for peace;
And hoped to give some timely balm to these
Unhappy feuds which stab Verona to the heart;
A thousand furies spur cold tolerance till she fires;
The mischief done, we then must rest content
With that which hath no cure.

Teobaldo. What care I now for rivalry of kin?
In the chill gloom of yonder silent vault
Otavio sleeps with those who've gone before;
A simple stone doth mark the spot; alas! alas!
In the spring of youth and beauty there he lies.
Oh, daughter, if the winged winds shall waft
Yon traitor Montes to another shore, for life,
Already hath the signal sounded deep for strife.
Otavio lies entombed, his cloak around his corse,
Awaiting his revenge, so I'll with speed
Proclaim to all our house the horrors of this deed.

Enter FESENIO.

Fesenio. Already have our band the slayer sought,
They say he posts to Rome in haste,
Our Duke gives escort to Ferrara's walls,
So as to stem our fury of assault.
The common cry, that time shall chill
The boiling blood of Castelvine's kin.
The people shout, young Montes drew
But in his own defence. And being true,
All blame Otavio, who with venom'd haste
Did seek the brawl, and knowing this
Have sheathed their swords in peace.

Teobaldo. No more, I am not marble, nor
My soul of adamant, my grief of heart
Is deep enough without thy stinging blame.
For hug I not my woe both night and day.
Oh, cowards, traitors, shameless rabble, say !
What, shall I die and have not my revenge ?
How well cold worldly comfort sounds to one
Who hath just kiss'd the dead cheek of his son !
Why doth hot vengeance sleep ? So old, so weak,
I'll to the Duke, and for this outrage seek
Some quick redress. Oh that my soul were free,
Otavio slain and dead, life hath no joy for me.   [*Exit.*

Dorotea. 'Twas barbarous thus to speak
Such words to one so stricken and so sad.

Fesenio. Lady, I wear the humble garb of service, yet
No truth nor honour have I lost ;
All blame upon thy brother rests.

Dorotea. I mourn my brother with a sister's grief,
And yet thank heaven that this Montes lives.

Fesenio. A Castelvin, and speak thus of our foe?

Dorotea. The daughters of Verona do esteem
Roselo Montes much, we Castelvines too
Admire his noble presence, and he's brave.
Methinks our Julia's eyes did brighten oft
As he did pass along.   [*Drums without.*

Fesenio. I hear the drums, some edict they proclaim.

Dorotea. Go learn the cause, I fear some evil
Greater than before.

SCENE II.—*An Orchard by* ANTONIO'S *house*.

Roselo. Hast well secured our ladder cords?

Marin. Sir, all is secure.

Roselo. At last we're 'neath the orchard wall!

Marin. My love and duty found me wings;
Am I not watchful ever to defend thee,
Should aught of danger or mishap surprise?
He who of little value holds his life,
Hath naught to fear in love or strife.

Roselo. Thy love for Celia, not for me:
'Tis that which makes thee bold and venturous.

Marin. Thou see'st my love divided;
One half for her, the other half for thee.

Roselo. As I sweet Julia come to woo, so thou,
To bid a long farewell to Celia comest now.

Marin. Well, that is true; but Celia's love
Could not alone have drawn me here, the dove.
But now I see thee safe beyond the wall,
I cannot but admire such love and constancy;
For how we came so safely and unknown,
So easy and unharm'd, I know not.

Roselo. I but my destined path pursue,
And yet I fear to lose my love so true.
  Marin. I hear the noise of footsteps coming pit-a-pat.
  Roselo. Look that our swords be ready to our hands!
  Marin. I breathe again ; there's naught to fear,
'Tis but the plashing fountain that I hear.
  Roselo. Julia, my heart's sole idol, comes this way!

Enter JULIA *and* CELIA.

Julia. My love, my husband !
  Roselo. Kind heaven, grant me firmness at my need,
For what would life's pulsations be to me,
Losing the kindred throb of thine, O Julia ?
Love, fond wife, in hope, in joy, despondency,
Or bitter grief, whatever ills befall, I'm arm'd.
Thus as I press thee trembling to my heart,
In absence still, in fancied presence thou ;
If those dear eyes rain tears at fortune's frowns,
Crosses or evil tidings touch of woe ;
Oh, kill me not by weeping now, sweet wife !
If thou desirest death, my love, one sword,
One blow, shall give our hearts' blood to the earth !
Those who now seek our lives may slay ; but still
Our souls shall live unparted after death !
Oh, sad and luckless feud ! Though guiltless I,
A thousand evils had I suffer'd with content,
Rather than kill Otavio, whose unruly tongue,
The quickening cause, alas ! of his untimely death,
More tears my life ! And if thou lov'st him dead
More than thy living husband, let this cursed hate,
Knowing no respite, die with me !

Take this poignard, plunge it in my heart,
And with my blood so end this hated strife.
Thou speakest not!

 Marin. Sweet Celia, should hot anger move thy heart
That I, faint-hearted, kept aloof from strife,
And mounting to the tower's topmost height,
Did shout, I but a peaceful friar am, and so
Did bring some scandal on the Church below,
In double-quilted doublet here I stand,
And here's my dagger ready to your hand;
Kill me, and then to prison go! Thou'rt silent, sweet.

 Julia. She who abandons all things for thy love,
How mourn a cousin while a husband lives?
I care not if the blood of all our house be shed!
I know no father, kindred, home—to me they're dead;
All, save one in whom my soul all worship knows.
Thou art my kindred—no Castelvin daughter I!
Once I bore that name, but now I Montes am
In hope, in thought, in soul and name!

 Celia. Most sweet Marin, for thee I now forget
I ever had a kindred, house, or name.
What care I if our linen washes white or no,
Or see the glass which holds our honied sweets
Be cracked or no? Why should I wish Marin
Were bold and valiant, risking precious life
In foolish broils? for fighting thou might'st
E'en meet death, and I a weeping widow be.
I'd have my lover to be this: in will
A game old fowl, wary, tough to kill.
The coward should most careful counsel know;
The brave and reckless can in useless broils show,
Keeping stern, wrinkled Justice all agog,

I

The city full of shouts and brawls.
I love you more than all my other loves ;
And as each hen doth wisely guard her nest,
So mine's well fill'd with jewels of the best.
The cocks may strut, and crow, and fight ;
Who cares ?   And shall I kill my loving knight,
By slipping steel 'neath doublet to his heart ?
Oh no !   I'll give instead the keys to open vaults
Well stored with rosy wines ; of that red blood
I give thee leave to drain full cups ; no other cares
Thy Celia dear to spare.   Oh sweet Marin,
Thine is the kindred and the house I love,
For in the flesh I Celia am, I know,
But in the spirit nothing but Marina.

 Roselo.   What would my own sweet love that I
In this perplexing strait attempt ?

 Julia.   In secret to Verona come when only stars
Can see, till favouring sunshine smiles with hope
Upon our loves.   Then fate shall waft us on
To Venice ; thy corded steps will point the way,
And my poor heart not even cold content can know
Until thou com'st again, husband, I love thee so.
Say thou wilt come, and quickly, too, ere I let thee go.

 Roselo.   Can my sweet Julia doubt her husband's love ?
Pray heaven that my father's face I no more see,
Nor be at peace with kindred of our house
Amid these broils and most accursed strife,
Or reach Ferrara's gates with life,
Or that some Castelvins may in ambush lie,
And rushing forth, stab till thy husband die ;
And so each hope of joy and bliss may fade,
Ere I one syllable omit of promise made.

Celia. And Marin, I know the loving one will come
To see and coax his Celia. Art thou dumb?

Marin. If it please heaven I no hindrance find
Upon the road, nor yet within the inns,
Nor want plump partridge for my evening meal,
Nor sound white wine to wash it down,
Why, then, if I do aught, my lovely maid,
Which harm may bring on me, I know
Thou wilt forgive Marin. And so my dove
Remember, be thou steadfast in thy love.

Celia. Not quite so steadfast as a running wheel,
A breeze, a summer cloud, a rolling dice,
I will remain, so long as brave Marin
Shall truly love his Celia.

Antonio (within). Lucio, good Lucio, my halberd bring,
I hear strange voices by the wall.

Julia. My father speaks without, sweet love.
Begone!

Roselo. See thou, Marin, the ladder now is sure.

Marin. Jump, master mine.

Celia. Stay, dear Marin; thy Celia speaks.

Marin. No staying now, sweet maid, for me.

Julia. Roselo, love, hast thou no guard?

Roselo. Ay, love, a good and true one, too.

Julia. Whom?

Roselo. Anselmo, with six trusty friends.

Julia. Farewell, sweet love. Once more, farewell!

Roselo. Farewell, my life and sweetest love!
Fear doth give thee wings, Marin.   [*Exit* ROSELO.

Celia. Oh, Lady Julia, thy father comes, I fear;
To even whisper now he's near

Enter ANTONIO, LUCIO, *and* TEODORO.

— *Lucio.* The footsteps sounded by the wall.

Antonio. Fire !

Julia. Hold, sir !

Antonio. Who goes there ?   'Tis Julia's voice !

Julia. I am that sad and hapless maid.

Antonio. Who spoke with thee anon ?

Julia. Celia, sir, is here.

Antonio. Why so late abroad ?

Julia. Have I not cause to be abroad, and with despair
To weep Otavio's cruel death
In red-eyed silence with the stars ?

Antonio. Sad tears and sighs can never bring
The dead again to life. so poets sing.

Julia. Wouldst thou have me insensible as stone—
Cold, bloodless as the marble statue of a maid ?
Weep I not Otavio dead—a husband in the cold tomb laid ?

Antonio. A husband !

Julia. He should have been ; and as a woman,
Marvel not I weep a husband dead.
'Tis good, and holds fair reason for my tears.
Revenge is quick, and like the jewel shines ;
'Tis bright, but hath no soul to feel ;
Pray heaven that this deadly hate or worse
End not with a father's death or curse !

[*Exeunt* JULIA *and* CELIA.

Lucio. Poor girl, alas ! she weeps.
Did she not in all heart-sadness say,
'Twas thy hot vengeance did a husband slay?

Antonio. In sorrow did I mark each word she spoke,
And though a husband she hath lost, her father lives.

Oh, had I known how much she loved
Otavio, I'd not have clamoured for revenge,
And wedding her, let vengeance sleep.
It grieves me sore to see her weep
Otavio dead, the more that all her tears
And woe be of a widow'd bride ;
I fain would see her lock'd in bonds of love.
Her husband should be brave and noble, rich,
And must well favour'd be.
Count Paris did entreat me for her hand,
Ere he did journey with the Duke ;
He will return anon.   Think'st thou, good Lucio,
She'll mourn the dead for ever, while
A living lover woos her tearful eyes to smile ?
- *Lucio.* Count Paris is a fitting and most proper lord
For so gentle gracious and so sweet a maid
As Lady Julia.
I pray you seek her, sir, and with most gentle words
Discourse of this most noble Count, whose sighs
Perchance will find some favour in her eyes.
      Antonio. A husband dead is mourn'd as cloudy day ;
Let sunshine on the morrow break, 'twill hap
You'll seek the grief in dark oblivion's lap.

SCENE III.—*The open country ; road leading to Ferrara.*

Count PARIS, ROSELO, MARIN, *and attendants.*

Paris. Our meeting thus indeed is sad.
No hatred know I for thy kin or thee ;
And when hath even busy rumour said
That Paris sided with Castelvin's lords?
      Roselo. If I, so desperate in my need, so sad,

Could much discourse enlarge,
Well might I of thy courage speak.
So of bright hopes all hunted from my heart ;
But I am forced to doubt all save fast friends ;
My reason and my heart have been at war.
I go, Sir Count, my sad and gloomy way—
It seems the way to night, and shames the day :
My only hope to die ;
And yet the death I seek I fly,
Yet, craving death, I am but coward clay,
As much as they who seek in hot revenge to slay.

    Paris. To aid thee in thy present peril now,
Doth with my anxious wish most firmly hold :
I count it gain that I have met thee here,
To hold thee free from every treacherous aim ;
And though my loving friend hath fall'n
Beneath thy deadly steel, yet do I know
'Twas in most fair and open fight ; and all
The justice thine, the provocation his.
'Tis true fair Julia I had hoped to woo,
And so my court I paid as Castelvines' friend,
But finding from her lip and eye she loved me not,
To press my suit had been to tempt blind love
To course most counter to my future hopes.
So now I no Castelvin am, for thee alone
Will even be a Montes, urging this feud
To some quick peaceful happy end.
If that thou carest, I to Ferrara's walls
Will go at once ; I turn me from Verona's halls.

    Roselo. Count Paris, well thy actions show
In my mishaps a noble friend,
True princely blood doth course thy veins ;

I hold myself thy debtor much,
And so remain your thankful slave.
From this fierce feud thy goodly sword
May aid to hold me free ; I ask no more
'Tween this and famed Ferrara's gates.
No cause have we to fear ; indeed,
Verona holds you much in need,
And in thy person hopes to quell these brawls.
I heard that suit of thine was made
To one of Castelvine's loveliest maids ;
Yet as a Montes now I hold thee friend,
And these brave deeds of thine commend.

 Count. Hush !   I hear the feet of strangers near.
 Roselo. Who goes there ?

Enter FESENIO.

 Fesenio. Señor, your name ?
 Paris. The Count of Paris.
 Fesenio. To thee, Sir Count, this letter now is charged.
 Paris. Fear naught, Roselo ; I am thy friend.—
From whom this letter ?
 Fesenio. Antonio Castelvin.
 Marin (*aside to* ROSELO). Pray stick the bearer, and at
  once !
 Roselo. Unharm'd he shall depart from hence.
 Marin. The words, no doubt, are full of peace—
The deed to kill us on the road.
 Roselo. For me, I care not what Fate gives ;
He dies with cheer who sadly lives.
 Marin. (*aside to* ROSELO). He seems much troubled as
  he reads.

Roselo (aside to MARIN). Mayhap they seek his friendly
    help
To slay both you and me.

Marin (aside to ROSELO). I feel we're dead, unless at once
We stick this fellow where he stands.

Roselo. What! would you thus defenceless slay
One who comes with courteous speech?

Marin. A plague upon all courtesies, I say;
I cannot play my life 'gainst treachery to-day.
He who doth love his kin may courteous die,
And yet, being dead, what worth his courtesy?

Paris. The words here written read,
And know the purpose of this messenger.
Read, Roselo. Share my good fortune too,
And wish me joy. Yet though I wed
Castelvin's lovely daughter, still
I shall not cease to hold myself thy friend.

Roselo reads. Hah!

Paris. Read!

Roselo. "If aught can in such cankering grief console,
'Twould be thy presence here, most noble Count;
My house is thine, and waits thy coming to defend
Verona and the cause of Castelvin as well.
Rumour hath whisper'd how Otavio fell,
Slain by Roselo Montes' treacherous steel!
Otavio's blood cries daily for revenge;
All wish you here to succour and to aid;
Julia a husband waits—I a son-in-law elect."
Alas, alas! what words are these! undone!
Julia a husband waits, and I a son!

Paris. What makes thy lip to tremble so?

Roselo. If Julia Castelvin shall wed with thee,

Then in great strait am I ; and yet, ah, me !
What need to speak again ?   Thy letter take,
One Castelvines more but one more foe will make !
  Paris. Am I of blood so vile, that thou
Suspect'st this letter shall have work'd in me
Such change, that I should cease to stand thy friend ?
What, though fair Julia claim Castelvin blood,
Shall I the vantage take, as man with man,
And quit all courtesies of gentle life,
Because I take this lady for my wedded wife ?
Shall I forswear all truth and honour ?—nay,
Go, and as thou banish'd art from that
Fair city where my wedded hope doth lie ?
I freely speak, and good Fesenio, here,
Hath a most noble heart, I know,
And will report this meeting to his lord
In such judicious guise as may be fit, and see
Naught of disfavour happen unto thee.
  Fesenio. Count Paris, thy wishes are commands—
I do your pleasure gladly, for although
Castelvin born and nurtured, yet
I do respect Roselo Montes much.
  Paris. Adieu, Roselo. Heaven have you
In safe keeping 'till we meet again.
  Fesenio. Adieu, Marin.
  Paris (aside to FESENIO). Mistrust doth hold him in her
    iron thrall,
So that his tongue scarce motion makes at all.
  Fesenio. 'Tis true.
  Paris. The bravest of us feel a sudden shock,
When threatening death at heart doth knock.—

        [*Exeunt* PARIS, FESENIO, *and attendants.*

K

Marin. Heed you the dangers which surround us now ;
We have, I feel, a thousand deaths 'tween this
And fair Ferrara's gates to brave.
Pray kick away these phrenzies you call love ;
And as for sighs, pray give them to the air above.
Let Lady Julia wed anew, and if as wife she dares,
She'll wed, methinks, a double sum of cares.

   Roselo. Marry.   That she should marry !

   Marin. Good Heavens, how you shout !

   Roselo. Who could have dream'd that in such angel shape
The fickle, faithless woman dwelt ?
The angels move like quicken'd thought from pole to pole ;
Thou, Julia, like them dost course this sphere,
And flash as lightning down from heaven's vault
To lowest hell.   Unhappy me, to trust so much
Those eyes' most sweet discourse, deceitful
In their wondrous light and sheen—
Kindling bright hopes, and fanning fickle love
Which holds high centre in her melting glance,
So women's weeping eyes unstable water drop ;
My tears are water too, but cannot quench
The raging fire which doth consume my soul !
No, 'twas not madness thus to love,
For who can love as he who much esteems ?
Oh, thou sweet sad cause of all my woe,
Thy wondrous beauty did entrance me so ;
And though thy beauty nought can e'er outshine,
Thou didst so match high heaven in thy love,
That truth and beauty equal balance held.
Ungracious Julia !   Know'st thou on whom
Thy fickle heart is fix'd anew ?
Look that thou knowest him well ;

In truth he cannot love as I do love!
Ambition guides thy greedy father's choice,
And truth and honour only second stand :
He'd have thee wed where his ambition points ;
He hates the man who in fair variance slew
Otavio.   Paris now call'd, doth journey with high hope ;
He was despised, but now revenge may grow,
For, not like me, though noble be his blood,
He feels no rushing torrent of love's flood.
And thou wilt be his wife—my wedded wife!
Can I speak thus, and still hold pulse of life ?

   Marin. What need to shout so loud, good master mine ?
Prudence demands you silence keep.

   Roselo. Silence! and why keep silence, knave, I pray ?
When the moon hath horns, then madmen have their say !

   Marin. If, then, thy madness be confess'd, shout on.

   Roselo. Oh, Julia! hadst thou been banish'd too,
The world had then esteem'd thee none the less,
For titles are but merchandize, and scutcheons paint.
On mine escutcheon no golden coronet doth blaze,
And yet Italia's early kings did give me breath :
Bright hope remains—I know thou wilt repent.
Thou hast no pride in empty blazoned names
But that alone which doth the purest soul uphold.
What value scutcheons in the light of day ?
Let night's black darkness round the scutcheons play.
Wedded to Paris, most perfidious maid,
Heaven shall curse, I only dare upbraid ;
For he may hate to-day
Who yester even did most madly love!
Why thus so generous with thy love ?   Oh, say—
Why give a cause to curse our wedding-day,

Why make my hope of bliss a heartless jest !
Oh, Heaven grant the ills I know ne'er be
Such as to tempt my heart to bitter thoughts of thee.
   (*There are several blanks in this speech, which will account
            for the want of a proper continuity.*
An' this be thy revenge for that ill-fated blow
Which slew Otavio Castelvin.   Why not, my love,
Have stabb'd me to the heart ? oh ! Julia sweet,
Such had been gentle mercy, oh forgive,
Thou shalt not wed Count Paris while I live.
   Marin. Oh, pray be silent, for 'tis but silly fools
Who for revenge use lip and tongue as tools.
   Roselo. How have revenge in deeds ?
   Marin. I'll tell thee, when we're safely housed
Beyond Ferrara's gates.
   Roselo. How ?
   Marin. By seeking there new wives.
   Roselo. To thee such may some solace bring.
   Marin. Here there is danger ; come.
   Roselo. Ungrateful Julia !—can it be the curse of love
To strike the stricken ?—Come, onward move.

ACT III.

Scene I.—*A Room in* Antonio's *Palace at Verona.*

Antonio *and* Julia *discovered.*

Antonio.

THY words would almost tempt a saint
To forfeit life.

 Julia. Take it, 'tis thine—'twas thou who
   gavest it!

 Antonio. I say again, it is my wish
That thou dost wed the Count.

 Julia. The Count hath much offended in mine eyes,
He did not challenge in the fray,
But let Roselo Montes unmolested go his way.

 Antonio. The Fates protect him 'gainst the darts of death,
And darkest danger harms him not.

 Julia. Holding alone defence of cloak and sword,
That day he should have not escaped the Count.

 Antonio. Loved you Otavio then so much,
Thou wilt not wed the Count, because
That villain Montes lives.

 Julia. I did dissemble many days,
For my poor heart's sake. But now,

Resentment somewhat old, I dare
Not suffer shock of Montes' death or hurt.
Think it not lightness thus to speak ;
I am but woman, and of purpose weak.

   Antonio. Revenge may be as sweet to me
As e'er it is to womankind! As Paris' wife,
Thy hope more sure, in him our great
Defence must ever hold.   He, knowing
How thy wishes drift, think'st thou
No cunning chance he'll find to slay
This villain we most hate of all the Montes' kin?
My word is pledged—thou'lt be Count Paris' wife?

   Julia. Oh heavens! father!

   Antonio. Had I thy wishes known, I had not
Call'd the Count, nor written him to press
His wedded hopes with thee,
Nor in my letters named him son!
This have I done, and thus thou'rt pledged
To be Count Paris' wife!

   Julia. Alas! alas!   Poor me!

   Antonio. Thou dost forget a widow'd father's claim.
Why weep, and court such red-eyed grief?
I'm not thy foe, nor he who kill'd Otavio.
Remember, Julia, I have promise made ;
Castelvin's honour knows no taint nor shade.

   Julia (apart). Great Heaven, how I tremble. Dare I not
     die?
What fear I then?—thrice welcome death, oh! why?

   Antonio (aside). She's doubting still.   I know not what
To tell the Count.   *(Aloud.)* Oh, Julia!

   Julia.   Sir,
I am ready, and to-day, to wed the Count ;

Whene'er he cares to claim mine hand,
'Tis his!

   Antonio. Thou speakest bravely.

   Julia. Sir, 'tis vain to seek to cross thee more :
Thine honour is as dear to me as is mine own.
Already call me, sir, Count Paris' wife.

   Antonio. My heart brims o'er with grateful love,
And knows a double joy!   Thy dower, girl,
It shall be great—thy mother's part,
In diamonds rich and rare ; the whole at good
Six thousand ducats priced !   The Count,
Thy husband, too, shall for his purse
Share full six thousand ducats more.

   Julia (*aside*). Each moment do I die a hundred deaths !

   Antonio. I go, my child, to see that all in order runs :
The parchments shall be drawn to-night !

   Julia (*aside*). What poisonous draught can half as deadly
      be
As that sharp grief which doth encompass me ?

   Antonio. Fesenio here !   Fesenio, quick, go bid our kin,
And say this wedding is a joy for Castelvin.   [*Exit.*

   Julia. Portia did seek stern death in stifling flame ;
Lucretia's steel was sharp and quick ; Dido with sword
At breast, sighed sweet memories 'neath the moon
To her brave Trojan youth, weeping salt tears
To swell the sapphire sea ; Iphis a cord
For blind Anaxaretes' love, and for that cold
Proud Roman's threat the subtle poison'd
Draught fair Sophonisba drain'd ;
Hero of Sestus on her sea-girt tower waits
Sadly in vain ; she sights Leander's corse,
And casts her body headlong in the surge ;

With poignard point at breast, and bated breath,
Slow sliding o'er the blood-stain'd grass
Dies Thisbe ; and so 'mid lovers holds
The palm for purest love.
For me, nor fire, nor cord, nor poison'd bowl—
One single shock shall free the deathless soul !

Enter CELIA.

Celia. With Aurelio, lady, did I speak, and in his hand
Your letter placed.

Julia. He read it ?

Celia. He did.

Julia. Scann'd he each word ?

Celia. Yes, dear lady ; and my grief was great
To see Aurelio weep, for at each word
He read, a bitter sigh escaped his breast.
His cell he enter'd, and when an hour had gone
Return'd, and in my hand this phial placed,
And said that thou should'st drink the juice
It doth contain.   So spake Aurelio, lady.

Julia. I did write that I would die by steel
Or cord, ere I, Roselo's wife, would Paris wed,
Celia, he knows our love, and knows that when
I penn'd those blotted lines, my life
Did hang upon a chance, and now distils
As comfort to my breaking heart nought
But some harmless sweet confection.

Celia. Thou knowest, lady, he's well skill'd
In subtlety of herb and poisonous weed,
And hath a fame more wide than all Verona holds.

(*Some lines wanting here.*)

Julia. He calls Roselo and myself his children.
(*Some lines wanting here.*)
He watch'd our growing love from earliest bud ;
True he is learned in every herb that springs,
And every subtle distillation, too, he knows ;
Should this be weak, and should its charm
Lead me to love the Count, and so Roselo harm ?
 Celia. To think thus, lady, is but witless wit.
He knows thy wedded hopes are new,
And ere he dare counsel thou shouldst wed again,
Would so have written by my hand ; `.`
No, as rare remedy for this hapless ill,
He sends this sweet confection still.
 Julia. Thou speakest wisely—say no more.
All evil when the body dies doth cease ;
I drink the draught ; Celia, farewell !
I die Roselo's own true wife ; this truly tell !
 Celia. 'Twill be but slumber, lady, soon we'll smile ;
'Tis but to give thee strength to slay
Such sad and luckless misery.
 Julia. Hah ! the confection works through all my veins;
My quaking flesh doth creep, my very soul
Seems torn from out its earthly home !
Oh Heavens ! some poison Aurelio hath distilled ?
Hast given me the potion that he sent ?
 Celia. That, lady, only which Aurelio did command.
 Julia. Methinks some sad deceit, and he
Hath changed the draught, the fluid works
Upon my bursting heart as rankest poison might.
 Celia. Didst drink it all, sweet child ?
 Julia. Each drugged drop, unto the last.
 Celia. What feel you now ?

L

Julia. That every vein doth throb and burst,
And every breath comes thick and hard ;
A crushing weight doth rest upon my heart ;
Oh heavens, Celia !

    Celia. Sweet lady !

    Julia. Madness now seems to seize my beating brain !

    Celia. What treachery's this ? Would I had ne'er been
      born
To be the messenger of ill, sweet girl ! !

    Julia. I would thou'dst brought it earlier. Oh, sweet
      sleep !
Tell my Roselo not my death to weep.

    Celia. Alas ! alas ! dear lady, I !

    Julia. Tell him I died his own true loving wife ;
Tell him I wait him 'mid the starry host ;
Tell him I died with woman's truth—
I could not live to be another's bride.
Tell him ne'er to forget his Julia—luckless maid !
Nor let her love e'er from his living memory fade.

    Celia. What cruel agony !—what moisture rests,
Like swollen dew-drops, on her gentle brow.

    Julia. My feet refuse their office—I cannot stand !

    Celia. Come, come, rest upon thy couch and sleep ;
'Twill soon pass o'er—let me lead thee in.

    Julia. I know not ! Oh, sad end to all my love !
And yet I die consoled—we'll meet above.
Celia, write tenderly to my husband when I'm dead ;
And—and——

    Celia. What says my Julia—mistress dear ?

    Julia. I know not what I spake. 'Tis sad to die
So young.

    Celia. Come, sweet lady—come, rest upon thy couch.

Julia. Father, adieu! I am Roselo's, and for ever now,
I'm his alone;—dear Celia, wipe my brow.

Celia. Come, gentle lady; come, I'll lead thee in.

Julia. I cannot stand! Oh, farewell, my husband!
My only love! sweet husband. Ah!   [*Exeunt.*

SCENE II.—*Street in Ferrara.*

FERNANDO, RUTILIO, *and Musicians.*

Fernando. Here we may sing.

Rutilio. Behind yon envious grate there shines
A wondrous golden sun, which gleaming gilds
And dazzles as the burnish'd ray
That from the eastward springs at early day.

Musician. The story runs, a stranger here hath fallen,
Enamour'd of this sun, and she so bright
With tender glances feeds his ravish'd sight.

Fernando. Comes he from Verona.

Musician. So goes the rumour here.

Fernando. Know'st thou his name?

Rutilio. Roselo!

Fernando. Hath Heaven endowed him with such gifts
Of grace and speech, that every woman's heart
Drops as ripe fruit when touch'd, into his lap,
While common chatter is so busy with his name?

Rutilio. Yes; but wise men would hardly care
To follow thus and such great peril share.

Fernando. Enough. I understand.

Rutilio. I know the Castelvines' kin in secret do
Pursue with cunning unto death this Montes youth.

Fernando. A vain enterprise 'twould seem.

Rutilio. In open fight Otavio Castelvin he slew,
Since then he goes so sad of face, I hardly dare
Be jealous of his love, or care.

Fernando. Let the musicians sing.

Rutilio. Hold! Some persons here approach
By yonder street.

Fernando. Strangers in Ferrara, too, methinks.

Enter ROSELO *and* MARIN, *without observing* FERNANDO,
RUTILIO, *and the Musicians.*

Marin. What news of love, my master dear?

Roselo. I but an unletter'd student am,
My earliest lesson has been conn'd in blood.
My soul is not of adamant. The sting
Hath enter'd deeply; the wound is fresh,
And bleeds.

Marin. So, if the fair Julia a second time shall wed,
This moonish madness should no longer fill your head.

Roselo. If high Heaven's angels smile on love,
Then dare I ask fair justice from above.

Marin. No doubt the angels straightway now will grant
Each tittle of the justice that you want.

Rutilio (aside to FERNANDO). That is Roselo Montes!

Fernando. Were we of Castelvin's kin, we might
Now find occasion free and opportune to-night.

Rutilio. Approach Fernando,
And close question seek.

Marin (aside to Roselo). Some fellows now approach, and
        see,
They watch us closely, too.

Roselo. Sirs! We are strangers, wand'ring through

Ferrara's streets, and seek the public square.

 Marin (*aside to* ROSELO). Thou hast done well, or all the town

Will in a twinkling follow on our track.

 Fernando. The public square, Sir Stranger, is

Hard by the street now facing this.

 Roselo. For your most courteous speech, good sirs,

We thank you much, and by your leaves,

Now pass on.

 Fernando. By yonder street doth run your way.

        [*Exeunt* ROSELO *and* MARIN.

 Rutilio. If this Roselo Montes be, the valour

Which high lineage gives is greater

Than thou dreamest.

 Fernando. So many seek his luckless life,

No wonder if he's armèd for the strife.

 Musicians. Shall we now sing, most noble sir?

 Rutilio. Nay, Silvio; for methinks I hear

The clash of naked steel, and near.

 Fernando. The feet upon the silent stones resound,

As dying thunder echoes o'er the ground.

 Rutilio. Unscabbard, then, your sword.

 Musicians. Let us, then, draw and seek the fray;

Guitars in such a case be out of tune. Away!

 Rutilio. And a poor target too; 'tis nought

'Gainst a Toledo blade, as sharp as thought.

 Musicians. A good thick wall's the better shield. [*Exeunt.*

 Enter ROSELO *and* MARIN, *with drawn swords.*

 Roselo. Well, didst thou feign a quarrel, good Marin?

Marin. And there they run for freshest news ;
The fruit of knowledge being well-worn shoes.

> [SYLVIA *appears at the balcony.*

Sylvia. Good gentlemen, what means this fray ?

Roselo. Go, good Marin, and tell their names.

Sylvia. Hist ! hist ! gentlemen, I pray.

Marin. Senor, 'tis you the lady from the balcon calls ;
I am a man, no gentleman within Ferrara's walls.

Roselo. What would you, lady ?

Sylvia. Who are the fellows to this noisy brawl ?

Roselo. If thou wilt listen, I will tell thee all.

Sylvia. I thank thee, stranger.

Roselo. Know, then, fair lady, we are twain
Who with our rapiers did prevent
A most unseemly brawl 'tween six
Who, coming here to sing beneath
Thy lattice high, we've chased them hence,
And now return to hold us at command.

Sylvia. Who, then, art thou ?

Roselo. Roselo Montes, at your feet.

Sylvia. Most welcome, sir ; but 'gainst six,
Thou didst then hold audacious odds.

Roselo. Then thou dost owe us thanks, fair Sylvia,
For being thus audacious in thy cause.

Sylvia. What news dost from Verona bring ?

Roselo. Ah me ! 'tis this. Julia Castelvin weds.

Sylvia. And thou dost sigh so deeply—why ?

Roselo. I sigh'd because mine enemies are strong,
And having little faith in Julia's love for long.

Sylvia. It grieves me sore to see thee heavy-hearted go.

Roselo. My grief is deep, and yet I glory
In such depth of woe for love.

Enter ANSELMO.

Anselmo (aside). They tell me that Roselo Montes here
Doth rest within some inn.

Marin. Their fool's errand o'er, they now return
To sing beneath her lattice here.
Come, let us say farewell and go.

Roselo. Dear Sylvia, now these brawlers do return ;
Hold thou no converse, but such fellows spurn.

Sylvia. Farewell.   I close my lattice for the night.

[ANSELMO *retires apart.*

Marin. So master mine, and what the whispers
'Neath the lady's lattice sigh'd ?

Roselo. Nought know I, and nothing care to know.
I cannot step but death doth gape,
With open jaws and hideous shape.

Marin. If here no rapture thou dost know,
Pray, let us to the snug posada go.

Roselo. In hoping thus to play with pain,
I know I mortal am ; the griefs of life
Do smart and sting, I wince at every step.
Oh, Julia, with blind love I fight,
Whose only aim 's to blind me with thy light.

Marin. Some one approaches !

Roselo. I would he carried bare the sword of death,
And so would ease me of my pain and breath.

Marin. Who goes there ?

Anselmo. His name who asks ?

Marin. Having no errand here, I pray
Your grace will walk another way.

Anselmo. Your graces, here remain secure.
I seek a stranger.

Roselo. Methinks that voice holds a most familiar sound.
Whence come you, sir ?

Anselmo. Verona is my home, but in Ferrara now
I seek a friend.

Roselo. 'Tis he !   Anselmo, mine own fast friend.

Anselmo. Art thou Roselo ? nay.

Roselo. Alas ! in truth I'm he.

Anselmo. Good fortune smiles on me to find
Roselo opportunely here.

Roselo. What news dost bring ?   What stirs
Within Verona's walls ?

Anselmo. News of complexion startling and most strange
This moving world ere knew !

Roselo. How—the Lady Julia weds ? is dead ?

Anselmo. No.

Roselo. What strange events can happen then for me,
If Lady Julia still unwedded be ?

Anselmo. From first to last the history thou shalt hear.
And, in the telling, neither pain nor woe ;
But step by step shall know the cause
That brings me here.

Roselo. Give thy news voice, and as we go
I'll listen.   Come, let us to the inn.

Anselmo. Listen !

Roselo. Breathless, agape, I wait thy wondrous words.

Anselmo. Antonio to his daughter did propose
This marriage with the Count ; but neither
His commands, the gentler sway of friends,
Nor word of kinsmen could persuade her aught
To sigh the magic " Yes."
Her father, using high authority and sway,
Perforce she yields, and, the betrothal fix'd,

The night did see the vestures of brocade
And gold in hottest haste prepared.
The torches lighted, Paris by her side attends,
When Julia swoons as one with mortal sickness struck,
And falls as dead.

 Roselo. What! my own sweet Julia dead?

 Anselmo. Hush! I did due caution hold, and said
That thou shouldst listen. She fell as dead.

 Roselo. How can I listen if my love lies dead?

 Anselmo. Thy Julia lives.

 Roselo. Doth she but live, Anselmo, then
I live, and love, and hope.

 Anselmo. Throughout the night her kin and friends
Did mourn and weep her sudden death;
The city, on the morrow, blank with grief did see,
Both young and old move sadly through the streets.

 Roselo. Go on. I long for daybreak and the light.
The morning sun to slay that bitter night.

 Anselmo. Slowly the day did break while Julia
As cold marble lieth on her couch.

 Roselo. What words are these? The daybreak comes not.
If my Julia still be dead
'Tis blackest night for ever.

 Anselmo. The next day pass'd, and, believing in her
  death.—

 Roselo. Oh! Anselmo, if this day pass not quickly
I, too, shall woo the icy chill of death.—

 Anselmo. At even-tide, 'mid bitter tears,
They bore her to the tomb.

 Roselo. What hope for me, Anselmo, if
My Julia lies entomb'd among the dead?

 Anselmo. Such weeping crowds were never seen before

M

Within Verona's walls.   Each one did go
With downcast eye and silently all grief and woe.
The youths and maidens follow close the bier ;
The old men, too, in vain repress the tear.

   Roselo. Why poison thus my anxious soul ?

   Anselmo. Listen !

   Roselo. Listen, say'st thou ?   Either thou art mad,
Or I some comprehension lack.   Why juggle thus ?
Julia dead, and then entomb'd,
And thou say'st listen ?

   Anselmo. Such wond'rous history as I shall relate
Was never heard till now.

   Roselo. I did rejoice when thou didst say she wedded not.
Think'st thou I do so now, my angel dead ?

   Anselmo. Listen !

   Roselo. What need, if Julia be entomb'd ?

   Anselmo. Much.

   Roselo. Like some grave leeches, thou, Anselmo, doth
By letting blood, drain ebbing life by drops,
Thus killing hope and slaying step by step.
My grief will gulph my reason soon.
Go on—what more of Julia ?

   Anselmo. Much ; and that of great import, too.

   Roselo. If there be one drop of comfort in the rest,
I will be calm, and listen patiently.

   Anselmo. The good Aurelio at this time did seek me out
To speak upon this matter ; these his words :—
How Julia, writing in perplexity, recounts
Her sad adventure and her bitter woe ;
And at the end these words were writ :—
Ere thou this letter will have read,
My dagger shall my heart's blood wed.

The good Aurelio did prepare a certain drink,—
And gave it with injunctions to her maid,
Saying it contained most potent means
Of poisonous and sweet subtle herbs,
The drinking which would bring two days and nights
Of deathly slumber to the heart.
Julia did drink it ; and Aurelio bade
Me come to seek thee here, and say
She lies entomb'd, in sleep's stern semblance
Silent death, within the vaulted tomb
Where rest the ashes of Castelvin's kin
(The body of Otavio resteth there).
Thy Julia sleeps ; go, and when she wakes again
Together fly, and dwell in France or Spain.

   Roselo. I tremble at thy words, Anselmo.   Should
She awake amid the silent trappings of the dead,
While we can scarcely, winging way through air
Be at the church ere she awakes,
Will she not die of fear ?

   Anselmo. Fear not ; Aurelio will be well prepared.
Come.

   Roselo. Marin, what thinkest thou ?

   Marin. Think ? that my fears do make me dumb,
And scarce allow my shorten'd breath to come.

   Roselo. Was I, then, born to show the gaping world
How much misfortuned love doth grow on hope ?
O Heaven ! why a moment stay
While Julia waits the dawning day ?

   Marin. A moment, sir, I pray.

   Anselmo. What seek you ?

   Marin. That vault you named, pray doth it hold
The bones of many dead ? and is it cold ?

Anselmo. Truly, of many, and 'tis somewhat cold.

Marin. Then, sirs, I care to hear no more,
But will e'en wait your worships at the door.   [*Exeunt.*

SCENE III.—*Room in the Palace of the* LORD *of* VERONA.

COUNT PARIS, *in mourning, and* LORD *of* VERONA.

Paris. From out this sable grief no gleam
Of dawning gladness dare I even dream.

Verona. He who reasons with discretion, Count,
Will find that Fortune rests upon a globe.
The mounting waves do ripple at her feet,
Now shouting with the storm, now smiling in the calm:
And thus dame Fortune leads us on to death,
Crowns evil with success, and joy doth nurse with woe.

Count. Sir, I am well advised
That were I master of a thousand worldly joys,
And by her fickleness did lose them all,
I'd laugh as loud as Democritus e'er did.
But that sweet angel now lies dead
Who made me joyous for a day—sweet bride !
The city mourns her as a sister dead.
My courage limps beneath the pressure of my woe.
Had she but lived a year—a month—
A week—a day—some consolation I might know
In place of anguish deep :
But holding thus the heavy hand of woe,
The force of fate doth bear me on to where
Death's silent shadows fall.   To bear
Such woe doth need a heart of bronze.

Verona. 'Twas wisely order'd from above.

Had it been a year—a month—a week—
A day—as love grew stronger so the pain
Should have grown more intense.
   Count. Oh, that such bliss had but been mine!
I cannot cheat my grief, the soul will pine.

Enter a Servant and ANTONIO following.

   Servant. With great Verona's noble Lord
Antonio Castelvin doth audience crave.
   Verona (aside to COUNT). See with what courage he doth
      bear his woe!
   Antonio. I come not, sir, to fill thine ears
With lamentations deep, nor yet with tears
To wring your soften'd hearts.   Nor tell
How much in error cruel Death hath been
To respite one whose life hath spann'd
Some steps beyond the goal.
'Tis said that Love and Death a journey went
In winter—I marvel much that Love should journey thus
With one who could so chill his loving heat,
For death is wintry cold.—Howbeit, they journey'd on,
Until the hostelry in sight, there lying down
They slept well past the midnight-hours:
Rising in the misty light exchanged their darts,
And bidding each adieu did journey on
Their separate roads ; and as they went,
Each fitted feathered shaft and twang'd his bow.
But after this the young men died,
And old men fell in love.   The interchange
Once made could never be annull'd.
In mine own house now 'tis seen, alas !
My daughter Julia dead.   Otavio, too,

Whom she did love, is lifeless clay,
My house is now a desert drear,
While I have great possessions ; so
That my kin would have me wed my niece,
Or all our names and wealth do die
With us.

    Count (apart to VERONA). 'Tis but a miser's artful tale.

    Antonio. I, who had hoped to know such sweet content,
My Julia wedded to this noble Count, and I
Arranged my bridal, too!   Poor Julia! child
Sleeping in the silent tomb! and so
The world doth go.   Ah me! ah me! and yet
Good Dorotea doth respond, and for our wedding seeks
A dispensation now from Rome.

    Verona. If, then, no chance there be to save these wide
        estates
But thou to wed fair Dorotea, thy closest kin alive,
She will in thee most surely find
One ever ready to consult each wish ;
For as Otavio and the Lady Julia now be dead,
So great a treasure for thy state as Dorotea is
Doth not Verona know.

    Count. I join you, sir, in every hope of joy ;
Mayst thou, Antonio, live both loving and beloved :
The heritage more seemly is, to rest with thee.

    Antonio. Not so ; still evil must be met.
I came to tell thee of these sad events,
Which, having fallen most crossly, thus
Do follow to their end.

    Verona. Time doth plough gently o'er thy brow,
Grey hairs should ever command respect.
Unseemly 'tis to speak of age whene'er

The bride is present.   All should then be mum.
  Antonio. Only to one who cares for face and youth,
But not to one who merit seeks and truth.
  Count. Such marks good reason for thy choice.
  Verona. Age and regret first cousins be.
  Antonio. Adieu! I go to visit my young bride.
  Count. With heavy heart I go—whate'er betide !

[*Exeunt.*

SCENE IV.

Sepulchral Vault beneath the Church of Verona.

Julia. Oh! where hath frowning Fortune led me ?
If I be dead, how sense of thought remain ?
So chill, so black, all murky night around ;
No door, no air.   Heaven denies me sight
Of his bright, pure, and glorious light.
Can I be sleeping 'mid the mighty dead,
And feel the chill of fading life upon my brain,
While yet stern will remains ? I know no pain.
Have I not flesh to feel, tongue, lips, and voice ?
What place is this, so dark, so foul,
So chill, so dank ? My very flesh doth creep.
Who, then, inhabit its dread silence ?   Sin-
Sickening corses seem to hem me in.
O heaven ! how I love sweet life !   Who, then,
Hath placed me living 'mid the dead, and when ?
Why gape these murky caves to gulf my soul ?
Stay ; mem'ry dawns ! the deadly draught
Aurelio sent hath work'd this chill, how then
Hold I still mysterious mortal ken,

How move, and feel, and think, and touch ?
Why shudder thus at chill of death ?
Yonder's the flicker of a flame, there yawns
The dark abyss, where mortal souls do mourn
Life's chances lost, that sad unfathomed bourn.
Hath Lethe's stream been bridged, and do I know
The pinching penalty of love and woe ?
The light approaches : if I be not lifeless now
I die of fear.

> *Enter* ROSELO *with a lantern,* MARIN *following.*
> JULIA *retires.*

Marin. Pray leave me here, 'tis more discreet,
I'll guard the door that's nearest to the street.

Roselo. Anselmo's there ; he will do all need.
Come thou with me. Why stand aghast, and look
So pale and tremble ?

Marin. 'Twere better that the Bishop and his train
Should come with holy water first.

Roselo. Ascend this step with care.

Marin. This step ! oh, dear !——

Roselo. Dost fear the silent air will eat thee ?

Marin. Ah ! I feel a touch upon mine arm !
   (*Overturns the lantern, and extinguishes the light.*)

Roselo. Accursed be thy clumsy hand and foot !

Marin. Assist me, Holy Mother, all the saints give aid.
I feel I'm dead and buried, with mouldy corpses laid.

Roselo. Silence ! some one speaks.

Marin. Oh ! did you hear a corpse's voice ?

Julia (*aside*). No doubt Aurelio's potion did contain
Some sweet confection wooing without pain,
Death's counterfeit, soft slumber.

And in this house of death they've laid me.

Roselo.   Again the whisper of a human voice.

Marin.   Oh, good San Pablo and San Lucas,
Et ne nos inducas.

Roselo.   Here, trembling fool, this lantern take,
And in the chapel of the church above
Thou'lt find a light.

Marin.   What say you, noble sir?

Roselo.   That thou hast heard me say.

Marin.   How can I venture there alone, for note you not
How unnerved I am?   I feel both cold and hot.

Roselo.   Cease thy coward words, and go at once.

Marin.   Good gracious!   who again hath touch'd mine
        arm?

Roselo.   Stay thou here; I'll go alone.

Marin.   What!   I stay here alone.   Oh, no!

Roselo.   What folly's this?   alone I go,
                (Here some lines are wanting.)

Julia (aside).   Methought that where I saw the dancing
        light,
I heard the sound of voices murmur near.
What!   do the dead speak, and do I living hear?

Roselo.   Hush!   hear you not a voice again?

Marin.   They say the blood doth course toward the heart;
Mine through the girdle, seems ready to depart.

Roselo.   The voice doth issue from that corner vault.

Marin.   Think you that chattering bony jaws can speak
Fair words?   No mouldy corpse would suffer such, I trow.

Roselo.   What can be done?

Marin.   How should I know?

Roselo.   Canst touch the wall?

Marin.   Ugh!   In the nape of the neck I've touch'd

N

A cold and clammy corpse, oh dear!
San Blas, Antonio, all the saints, oh, hear!
   Roselo. How now?
   Marin. Ugh! I touched it now; so fat and soft,
A friar's paunch, I'll swear. Ah, here's a skull!
It seems an ass's, 'tis so big: I feel
As if his teeth were fix'd upon my heel.
   Roselo. What!—teeth?
   Marin. I tremble, know not what I say or fear;
I put my finger 'tween the stones all broken here,
And thought 'twas something gnawing at my flesh—
Who touches me again—oh, dear!
   Roselo. Where have they laid Otavio's lifeless corse?
   Marin. Why speak of that just now, good sir?
Oh, help!
   Roselo. What now?
   Marin. Oh, mercy, why did I omit to bring
The indulgence snugly in my pouch?
   Roselo. For what?
   Marin. Did I not eat the missing trout, and all
The pears that lay in sugar, and swear I did not?
   Roselo. Have done thy senseless chatter.
   Julia (aside). Alas! alas! no hiding-place I see;
They come, alas! and whither shall I go?
Gentlemen, pray, say are ye alive or no?
                     [ROSELO *and* MARIN *fall down.*
   Marin. I'm not alive; in fact, I'm sure I'm dead.
   Roselo. Who speaks of death with such melodious voice?
   Marin. Indeed I'm dead. Let me 'scape this once,
And ne'er again will I come groping in
Cold, dank, and deathly vaults, on such fool's errand
As this same.

Roselo. Sweet Love, illumine with thy magic fire!

Marin. I wish Love would; these dead men here
Like droning bees go buzzing by your ear,
First right, then left, but give no light to cheer.

Roselo. Courage, we'll shout.   Sweet Julia, love!

Marin. We'll suppose Otavio hears you call
He'll wake the drowsy dead both great and small.

Roselo. My Julia, sweetest love and wife!

Julia (*aside*).   That voice!—it brings assurance to my
         heart;
But if it be Otavio's voice, I'll call,
And solve all doubt.   Otavio, speak.

Marin. They call Otavio, and we're dead men now.

Roselo. I'm not Otavio, nor his shadow'd self.

Julia. Who then art thou?

Roselo. Roselo Montes.

Julia. Roselo?

Roselo. Dost doubt?

Julia. Some token give in proof.

Roselo. Anselmo did advise me that, with cunning skill,
Aurelio had prepared some drink,
Which being drunken simulates still death.
He sends me thus to rescue thee,
That all being blinded by thy seeming death,
I may in silence bear thee from this vault.

Julia. What gave I on the night we parted?

Roselo. A precious relic, love and wife!

Julia. And thou to me?

Roselo. Two stones, in shape like hearts, and clasp'd
Tightly 'tween golden links.

Julia. And on the morrow?

Roselo. The diamond jewel which doth clasp my plume.

Julia. These tokens are most certain ; still
In my first letter what wrote I ?
   Marin. More questions in this murky, musty place !
   Roselo. To the husband of my soul !
   Marin. Oh, handsome Doña Nuña, say
Whether she be dead or nay ;
For 'mid the dead I'm often told,
Dwell neutrals, neither young nor old,
Who neither flesh nor bone doth hold.
   Roselo. Leave us, Marin.
   Marin. What presses now my noble lord ?
   Julia. Approach, dear husband of my soul !
   Roselo. Thy voice within my heart doth fading hope
      revive.
   Marin. All is accomplish'd ; now let grief
Again resume her sway, for as I'm dead as thief,
'Tis somewhat late to speak.
   Roselo. Out, blockhead !   Thinkest thou that I
Am quite as brainless as thyself ?
   Marin. Come, let us away, lest morning's dawn
Doth change to murky night.
   Roselo. Go whither ?   Say, sweet wife.
   Julia. It will be wise we still go well disguised ;
So long as these sad ills pursue,
At the farm which my dear father owns,
Two labourers' dresses will be good masquerade.
   Roselo. Thy beauty will peep out, and give the lie
To that coarse dress which may enshroud thy charms.
   Julia. What, when all do think me dead ?
   Roselo. Let us forth, sweet Julia.
   Marin. Wait !
   Roselo. For what ?
   Marin. I care not to go last—I'll lead the file.

Roselo. O Fortune fair, upon our true love smile.

[*Exeunt.

SCENE V.—*A Farm-house near Verona.*

Enter BELARDO *and* LORETO.

Loreto. I tell thee that I saw them all depart,
And they'll be here anon.

Belardo. Good lack, so many gentlefolk, the house
Will scarcely hold their lacqueys.

Loreto. Thou of the spade and sickle put aside
Thy farming books of how to sow, to plough and reap,
While I the news of this brave wedding do relate.

Belardo. For me, my son, more cares than joys
Must I expect ; but what wedding's this ?
For I but yestermorn did see the funeral's pomp.

Loreto. Out of that sad funeral, sir,
This very wedding is but newly born.

Belardo. How so, when all Verona weeps
That sad event ?

Loreto. Our Lord Antonio left alone to grieve
In sadden'd home the death of Lady Julia.

Belardo. True ; what then, Loreto ?

Loreto. His noble brother, too, doth own broad lands,
And holdeth it much value.

Belardo. Just so, my son.

Loreto. Having a daughter, Dorotea, he would wed
Her to her uncle, so the lands should own
No alien blood, and for the wedding feast
They from Verona come anon.

Belardo. Good ; the reason seemeth very good.
God help us then, and may the maid

Ne'er change to love some fair-hair'd youth ;
And pray no deluge comes to sink the lands,
When all would fail and need no holy bands.

   Loreto. Rather than that, I'd marry her myself.
   Belardo. Thou ?
   Loreto. Why not ?
   Belardo. A fine wife, truly ! and for thee, Loreto !
   Loreto. Is it not better she should wed with youth,
Than one who numbers summers twenty-nine
Just twice told o'er, good sir ?
   Belardo. Call Tamar here.
   Loreto. Tamar ! Tamar !

Enter TAMAR.

   Tamar. Ye shout as I were deaf.
   Loreto. Father but said, Go call Tamar,
And so I call'd.
   Tamar. He didn't bid thee shout.
   Loreto. Rather than see thee kicking idle heels,
I'd have thee married, Tamar dear.
   Tamar. Have me married ! Bah !
   Loreto. Why not ? Art thou a woman only in disguise ?
   Tamar. Didst thou call, sir ?
   Belardo. Here, make all clean in every room,
For all the world is coming to the farm.
   Tamar. What ! and the Lady Julia, too, just dead ?
   Belardo. Her father marries with his brother's child.
   Tamar. But why come here ?
   Belardo. See you not, that while they go seek from Rome
The proper dispensations for the match,
They do not care to stay within Verona's walls.

Tamar. Umph! high blood doth favour all;
No bad intention doth it seem, I wot.
Alone I cannot entertain so many guests.

    Belardo. Go, bring the readiest damsels on the farm to
        help.

    Tamar. So, so.

    Belardo. Come, then, Loreto, let us walk,
And waste not time in witless talk.

    Loreto. If I be witless, am I not thy son?

    Belardo. Mayhap I'm even witless as thou art.

    Loreto. In truth, a heart so warm and true,
So easy moved, there never was before,
Nor seen, nor heard, nor ever writ about.

    Belardo. I've lived according to mine age and wit.

                    [*Exeunt* BELARDO *and* LORETO.

    Tamar. This marriage—all the world gets married now.
All the world goes upside-down, I trow:
The young men to their graves, the old
To joyous wedding-feasts; the damsels sold.
I envy not the Lady Dorotea, for
I'd rather feed a starving hope than
Share so lame a feast, served up
With hairs as grey as winter's dawn.

Enter ANSELMO, ROSELO, JULIA, *and* MARIN, *disguised as
    villagers, with slouched hats, reaping-hooks, &c.*

    Anselmo. Peace rest upon this house.

    Roselo. God safely guard the lady of this house.

    Marin. Heaven prosper, too, its bread and wine.
Amen, I wish it was the hour to dine.

    Julia. And Heaven grant a sweetheart fair

To that young damsel, if not wedded yet.
Jaundiced envy touch all married ones,
And they who're not, may weep with rage in vain.

    Tamar.   Heaven bless you all, good folk !
Are you of this village, pray?

    Roselo. Ferrara is our native home.

    Tamar. Odds, life! take off thy hat and cloak, my
       child.

    Julia. All through the night we've journey'd on
Our cheerless, dull, and weary way.   Let me retire,
And anon I'll at your service be.

    Tamar. Now, which of ye three the damsel claims ?

    Marin. She should be mine.

    Tamar. You should look wiser, for her choice
Shows crabbed taste when two
Such pretty fellows did remain.

    Julia. And which wouldst thou choose,
Hadst thou the choosing now ?

    Tamar. The taller ; for his bearing and his eye
Doth promise love and wit and honesty.

    Roselo. Perhaps my companion here might be the wiser
      choice.

    Julia (aside). Although I feel his words to be but jest,
My heart owns pang of jealousy as passing guest.

    Tamar. O Heaven pardon me, my child !
Methinks I see my Lady Julia's look, sweet girl.
Come, what seek ye here ?

    Anselmo. Honest labour and its worth.

    Tamar. My father's in the fields, and with
My brother seeks some help to tend
Upon my lord, who comes with friends to-day.

    Julia. Comes your lord here to-day ?

Tamar. Our lady Julia being dead was buried too ;
She was the daughter of my lord ;
His brother's hopes now hang
Upon a marriage of their kin ;
So, while the Holy Father they do importune
For leave and licence of this troth,
The would-be husband does not care
The lady should in old Verona stay,
Lest she might find a younger love, and haste away.

 Roselo (apart to Julia). Hearest thou, sweet wife ?

 Julia (apart to Roselo). Ah, sad unhappy me !

— *Anselmo (apart to Julia).* Thy father then will wed again,
Thy patrimony lost, and I
Then left alone to pine without my Dorotea,
Whom I have loved since that sweet night
When mask'd we danced till morning's light.

 Julia (apart to Anselmo). Great Heaven ordaineth all things
As it will ;—
So, beauteous damsel, I in good time come
To aid thee in thy household need ;
These good men too their hands can try
Without upon the farm.

 Tamar. Then get thee into yonder chamber, child,
While these three fellows may
Be busied out of doors.

 Julia. Farewell, companions dear.

 Roselo. Adieu, Marcella, till we meet again.

 Anselmo. Adieu, adieu !

 Marin. A wondrous story ! 'tis most wondrous still ;
Shall all this loving end in joy or ill?

   [*Exeunt* JULIA, ROSELO, ANSELMO, *and* MARIN.

Enter ANTONIO *and* LUCIO.

Antonio. I fear me they are unprepared
To house of guests so large a troop,
And our coming is so sudden too.
— *Lucio.* Is it not better, sir,
That unadvised we come.
   Antonio. Tamar, Tamar!
   Tamar. Why, 'tis my lord Antonio, on my life.
   Antonio. Knows not your father of our coming?
   Tamar. The news of this brave wedding travels quick,
He doth approve, our only fear
'Tis somewhat hurried.
   Antonio. 'Tis by prevision that I do forestall
The foot of Time, I'm somewhat aged,
And Dorotea very young, but if delay
Prescribes a single year, our wedding day
Might never dawn.
I should most willingly have advised
You of our coming in such haste,
 But as ourbrother did command
That Dorotea should come hence to-day.
   Tamar. Perhaps he was wise, for she who weds
An aged grey-hair'd spouse, most surely looks
On brisk and black-hair'd youths as better cooks.
   Antonio. Am I so very old, good Tamar, then?
   Tamar. No, no, not very old; but if you scan
Your face before a mirror, then you can
Find some fair show of frosted hairs.
   Antonio. Go, Tamar, go, and all things have prepared.
   Tamar (apart.) Do but to an old fool speak of age,
He loses brains and temper, I'll engage.   [*Exit.*
   Antonio. Go, Lucio, see if all our friends be housed.

Lucio. I fly with wingèd heels, my lord. [*Exit.*

Antonio. Good Tamar, well I know in frosty age
This is excess, and still my hope's for one
Who shall succeed, and so inherit all.
This is no new creed I preach, and for the fault
I'll find a thousand pleas of exculpation;
Slowly creeps the shade of blacken'd night,
From lowly valley to the mountain's peak,
Within his chariot dark.

(*Some lines wanting here.*)

No reason this why Dorotea's coach
Should be benighted; a lover now would rave
In ecstasy; but grey hairs are more grave.

(*Some lines wanting here.*)

[*A noise is heard above.*

Preserve, me heaven, what noise is that?
Sure 'tis the thunder's echo that I hear!
It seems as if the wheels of sound
Had snapp'd their axles, and in one dread crash
Tumbled in atoms to the earth.
The strength of blood is not so sound
In creeping age as 'tis in lusty youth;
My hair doth stand on end in truth.

Julia (*unseen above*). Father, father!

Antonio. Great heavens, I know that voice, 'tis—

Julia. Father!

Antonio. 'Tis Julia's voice, or fear creates the sound.

Julia. Listen, ungrateful father mine,
If thou hast ears to hear; from out
Beyond the clouds of death I speak.

Antonio. It is indeed my Julia's voice!

Julia. Hast thou forgotten all, that thou canst doubt
Thy daughter's voice ?

Antonio. Where art thou, child, and what thy wish ?

Julia. From the bright world of seraphims I come
To hold discourse with thee.

Antonio. Sweet child, thy words I hear, but seeming night
Doth cheat me of thy face the sight.

Julia. Darest thou to look upon the form I bear ?

Antonio. No, I should die ; speak, say on.

Julia. 'Twas thee alone who caused my death.

Antonio. I caused thy death, oh heavens ! how !

Julia. Didst not seek to wed me 'gainst my will ?

Antonio. I did advise as seemed best.

Julia. Count Paris did deserve a noble bride,
But Love permits not wives to wed.

Antonio. The blame indeed was thine ; such tardy truth
As that thou now dost speak
Should have been then discoursed.
Oh Julia ! why not have prattled :—
Father mine, I am a weak and wayward girl,
Have set thy will at naught,
Love's fetters outweigh gold, both scales and all.
Thou shouldst have pardon sought,
I with thy falling rain of tears soon bought.
Thy choice would be of no ignoble blood, I trow,
For thou the Phœnix of all virtue art, I know.

Julia. Had my choice been of more ignoble blood,
I had thy blessing and forgiveness sought ;
But fortune gave me such a noble love,
I dared not.   To him Aurelio wedded me,
Breathing all holy blessings of the church ;
For two short months I knew this bliss.

Antonio. Were two months then so short,
Thou couldst not seek thy father's heart?

Julia. Oh, father mine! how could I dare?
Bewildered joy imagined dangers dark,
I saw myself a living wedded wife,
And thou wast bent upon another choice.
I sought still death, and now again
I speak, unseen unto thine earthly eye;
But father, thou wilt wedded be anon,
Accept a daughter's prayers, I'd have
Thee wed, forgetting me and all my faults;
But should my memory fragrance hold,
Forgive my husband, and in peace remain
For my poor sake; oh! seek not to destroy
The heart I love, or at each coming night
I'll hover o'er thy couch with torment, till the light
Compels me to be gone.

Antonio. His name?

Julia. Alas! 'tis he who did Otavio slay,
The son of one whose deadly hate thou know'st,
Roselo Montes he is call'd. Farewell!

Antonio. She's gone, Julia, Julia, daughter, child,
Darling of my heart! Roselo Montes,
Roselo, the name offends me so,
And yet I love the child so much, e'en he
Shall as thy husband honour'd be,
I'll hold him as my son for evermore.

Enter TEOBALDO, DOROTEA, COUNT PARIS, BELARDO,
   soldiers with halberds, ANSELMO, ROSELO *and* MARIN,
   as prisoners.

Teobaldo. Onward, accursed ones!

Antonio. What means this tumult, Teobaldo!

Teobaldo. Hail it as good fortune, and rejoice.
For heaven at last though slow
Some favour for revenge doth show.

Antonio. What people then are these?

Teobaldo. Know ye them not, spite all disguise,
This is Roselo Montes!

Antonio. Roselo here?

Teobaldo. Yes, indeed Roselo, and 'spite this disguise
Did heaven decree he should be known
By many of our people here.
I could have stabb'd him to the heart,
But give him o'er to thee;
Belardo, too, having no eyes to see,
Such servants of our house no more
Should hold the charge of this estate.

Belardo. Had I suspected this accursed foe,
No other hand had made his life blood flow.

Teobaldo. Consider we anon what death he dies;
Shall he be tied both hand and foot
To yonder tree, and each an arrow shoot?
Or will you slay him with thy sword or gun?
Speak, Antonio, and let the deed be done!

Antonio. Listen, Paris, Teobaldo, listen all.

Teobaldo. What death?

Antonio. He must not die; Roselo Montes is to live;
Julia in spirit now did speak
From just above this roof;
Her voice in sweetest heavenly accents sigh'd,—
I am Roselo's wife, for him and truth I died.

Teobaldo. Stay!   ·

Antonio. For why?

Fearing that force should press her choice,
And bind a hated marriage with the Count,
She sought from poison's subtle art
A quick and sudden death, and will
Torment my nightly slumbers still
With maddening dreams of hate and woe,
If I shall live Roselo Montes' deadly foe.

Teobaldo. Fancy, fear, or moonlight doth produce
Such sad disorder'd fancies of the brain.

Antonio. Brother, if still thou doubtest, even now
Mayhap she'll come and speak—I'll call.

Teobaldo. No, no, Antonio, let her stay,
I'll believe without a doubt each word you say.

Antonio. Roselo Montes was my son, is yours;
Then give him that rich prize, thy daughter here,
I care not now to woo fresh woes.

Teobaldo. My daughter, Dorotea?

Antonio. The same, and so this day shall peace
Be here confirm'd between our rival kins.

Count. So run events, that heaven's will
Declares how peace we may fulfil.
Teobaldo, now accept this noble youth
As Dorotea's husband, he's a man of truth.

Teobaldo. If peace by heaven thus shall be ordain'd,
Roselo take her as thy wife.

Enter JULIA.

Julia. No, not so; wouldst thou, traitor,
Wed two wives?

Dorotea. Julia!

Teobaldo. 'Tis she!

Julia. Let none depart.

Count. Julia, fair lady.

Julia. Father, behold thy erring child ;
I live to love thee as of yore.

Teobaldo. What would you, Julia ?

Count. Tell me, sweet wife !

Julia. Thy wife, Sir Count ! I am Roselo's,
His alone.

Count. I care not then to know thee.

Julia. Thou seest I am alive.

Antonio. Art thou alive in body or in spirit.
What wouldest thou ? care you
That we consign thee to the tomb again?

Julia. 'Tis true I living am, and in the flesh,
That simulated death was caused
By simples, subtle and most cunning,
Roselo Montes brought me here.   Speak,
Dear husband of my heart.

Roselo. Once rescued from the grave, she's twice
My wedded wife.

Count. And then twice over should she wedded be.

Antonio. My hand, Roselo ; and to thee, dear child,
My arms.

Julia. Wait, dear father, first my cousin there
Shall have the husband of her choice.

Teobaldo. And who is he, I pray ?

Julia. Anselmo.

Anselmo. And that is me ; I am prepared
With list of all my virtues, gold and gems
And lands.

Antonio. Enough, let's join their hands.

Marin. And I, with all my virtues, where
Shall I find one my cares to share.

The fright I had upon that awful day,
When I dragg'd forth from death yon mortal clay.
   Julia.   Celia is thine ; a thousand ducats too.
   Roselo.   Good senators, here, I pray 'tis understood,
The Castelvines ends in happiest mood.

FINIS.

CHISWICK PRESS :—PRINTED BY WHITTINGHAM AND WILKINS,
TOOKS COURT, CHANCERY LANE.